REVIEWS FOR *LAURENCE KLAVAN*

"I have this secret addiction to the short stories of Laurence Klavan...They are full of unexpected joys and leave me feeling terribly uneasy and blissfully satisfied."

—John Guare, Tony Award-winning author of *Six Degrees of Separation* and *The House of Blue Leaves*

"A playwright, graphic novelist and mystery writer, Laurence Klavan has long enthralled audiences with his extraordinarily fertile imagination, insight and style. He is also an admired short story writer."

—T. J. Stiles, author of the Pulitzer-winning *The First Tycoon: The Epic Life of Cornelius Vanderbilt*

"Laurence Klavan uncovers the places you didn't know exist, the gaps between everyday life and existential horror, where the disconnect between reality and the weird operates its quiet and subtle magic."

—Maxim Jakubowski, author, and editor of *The Mammoth Book of Erotica*

"Disturbing, surprising, and unflinchingly intimate, Laurence Klavan's stories make the mundane bizarre and are absolutely engrossing."

—Danica Novgorodoff, author of *The Undertaking of Lily Chen*

"Wonderfully strange tales—cunningly written—eerie and satiric by turn--often evoking tremendous pathos."

—David Greenspan, Obie Award-winning author of *The Myopia*

The Flying Dutchman

Laurence Klavan

Regal House Publishing

Copyright © 2026 Laurence Klavan. All rights reserved.

Published by
Regal House Publishing, LLC
Raleigh, NC 27605
All rights reserved

ISBN -13 (paperback): 9781646036714
ISBN -13 (epub): 9781646036721
Library of Congress Control Number: 2025937288
Cover images and design by © studiochi.art

The following is a work of fiction created by the author. All names, individuals, characters, places, items, brands, events, etc. were either the product of the author or were used fictitiously. Any name, place, event, person, brand, or item, current or past, is entirely coincidental.

All rights reserved. No part of this publication may be reproduced, stored in a retrieval system, or transmitted, in any form or by any means, electronic, mechanical, photocopying, recording, or otherwise, without the prior permission of Regal House Publishing.

All efforts were made to determine the copyright holders and obtain their permissions in any circumstance where copyrighted material was used. The publisher apologizes if any errors were made during this process, or if any omissions occurred. If noted, please contact the publisher and all efforts will be made to incorporate permissions in future editions.

Regal House Publishing supports rights of free expression and the value of copyright. The purpose of copyright is to encourage the creation of artistic works that enrich and define culture.

Regal House Publishing, LLC
https://regalhousepublishing.com

For Susan Kim

She got a shock; that's what Olive imagined when she kissed him. She knew it was impossible, there wasn't that kind of electricity, though this was as far as she could go, she'd always been a lousy science student. Olive only knew the guy was a 3D clone recorded by two lasers "interfering with each other," as a website said, a photographic replica, a facsimile, a hologram, he wasn't there, his performance had been recorded ages ago, she could not actually kiss his mouth and so not literally be shocked by doing it, as she might have been by rubbing her feet on a rug.

Yet it excited Olive to imagine it. She'd never admit it, but the idea of being singed by someone's lips aroused her. This was surprising, for she barely knew herself in this regard. Even though she was twenty, she was a young twenty; if age was determined by experience, in this area, she'd had very little, okay, almost none. Olive had learned she enjoyed imagining her lips being blistered by kissing Fyfe Moreso, pressing her real mouth on the hologram of his mouth as he had opened it months ago to sing a song that let him part his lips and extend his tongue, to sing the "l" in the word "love." The slightly shaky snow of his image, as people used to call rotten reception, made her think it had shocked her, especially when she sucked his tongue as she pretended to do now, alone in her room, pressing her face flat against the image, the idea, the holographic memory of his open wet red lips and mouth.

Olive had made sure her door was locked, because she feared being embarrassed—not just by being revealed to be sexual or sensual or whatever—by being exposed as immature, as younger than she was, as a teenager past her prime. For what was more teenage than loving Fyfe Moreso? He was the newest teen idol, the biggest in years, the one with the largest and most diverse audience, due to his constant shape shifting and massive mutability. He was impossible to pin down: his costumes ranged from a pirate eyepatch and a baby bonnet to an eighteenth-century corset and prosthetic stumps for legs. Some doubted he existed at all, unless they attended by lottery one of his streaming concerts, sitting in one of the few sections cordoned off for real people in mammoth and empty arenas. Yet Olive didn't care. He was utterly real in her arms today, a shimmering and crackling approximation of himself, pale, scrawny and hairless, like delicious drippy batter before it was baked and existed to be eaten.

Now Olive placed her pelvis against the image of

Fyfe's bottom half, pretended he was inclining, pushing and pulsing against her. They were "interfering with each other," as she spread her legs and sank her teeth into the lengthening and thickening erectile tissue of his electronic tongue, feeling she was about to have the first non-solitary orgasm of her life. She knew she was still alone if you were a stickler, but wasn't this better? Fyfe had been captured at his best forever, was both alive and non-existent, here and history, his image immediate and immortal as she moved and moved against it. Fyfe was about to know what she was like when she came, which no one else had ever known. Fyfe would know her truly as…

"Olive?"

Olive scrambled away from Moreso, who kept performing. She hurried to the button on her phone which would erase him from the large screen on which he was projected (it was bootleg footage in the first place). Her father's voice sounded urgent.

"Olive?"

Aware that her dad, Lorne, was in his own way as mercurial and high-strung as she, Olive didn't know how seriously to take him. Yet obeying an ancient instinct no amount of new technology could alter, she opened the door, which was a door in his large suburban house, where she still lived.

Her father stood shifting and sweating on her threshold. Like other wealthy men his age, he believed he didn't delegate and, at great personal price to himself, attacked all issues by himself.

"It's very important," he said.

Olive had been burned before, taking her father at his word when he spoke like this. Yet again, she was the servant of primal pressures she could not ignore.

"What is it?" she asked.

"It's about Fyfe Moreso."

Olive's mouth opened involuntarily. How had her father known about her dreams and imagined interactions with the star? Had he always? Did he wish to police or prohibit them? Why? Olive felt completely nude.

"That weak, wimpy clown," Lorne said. "He can't play my party. Not can't—he won't."

"What?"

Olive heard a mix of instability and petulance in her voice, which was new in a conversation with her dad. She was not just fearful of him but resentful, because he'd entered her dreams without asking. It gave her a power she could not yet control.

"The party," he said.

"What party?"

"The one I'm throwing."

"You're throwing a party?"

"I told you."

"You didn't."

"I'm telling you now."

"Well, what about…"

Being forced to utter Fyfe Moreso's name was like adopting a new public identity against her will. She wanted to do that in her own time. So, Olive didn't complete the question and let her father do it for her.

"…Fyfe Moreso?" he said.

Olive just nodded, which was less incriminating.

"He was going to be my coup de theatre," he said.

"Your what?"

"My big finish, my spectacular…you know, my way to…"

Now her father became the one who clammed up, unwilling to volunteer too much about himself, another way in which they were similar. Olive knew Lorne meant: Fyfe would have been his way to impress the neighbors, the world's biggest celebrity playing his private bash.

"But, no, Moreso had to be so greedy that…"

Lorne criticized Fyfe Moreso in the only ways he knew how. He mocked his name ("Torso"), then railed against the singer demanding his usual huge fee for a private appearance. He seemed to feel Fyfe should do it for free or even pay *him* for the privilege.

"Who does he think he is, the androgynous punk?"

Olive began to calm down. She realized her father hadn't discovered her obsession: he'd merely researched the latest and most lucrative craze he could rub in his neighbors' faces by presenting. If Fyfe had agreed to the offer, her dad would still have privately disparaged him. Since he'd said no, Lorne could openly mock him.

"He thinks he's someone beloved by billions of people."

Olive blurted out, "He is."

Her father stopped the agitated weaving he was doing on her doorstep. He seemed to suddenly perceive Olive, just in time for her to turn and avoid his perception. Then Lorne segued from being challenged by his daughter to being even more doggedly dismissive.

"Is it the baby bonnet?" he asked. "Or the fake no-legs? What do you like about him?"

"Never mind."

"Or is it his anorexia that makes him adorable?"

Surprising herself, Olive began to close the door on her dad. The spirit of the gesture tickled Lorne, who held it open while he laughed. Olive was relieved by his condescension. Considering her feelings about Moreso a foolish and endearing post-adolescent crush kept him from knowing the true nature of her devotion, which was too deep for even her to plumb. This allowed Olive to continue to start to know herself in peace. It was what she'd spent all her days doing after dropping out of college.

"Want these? Here."

Lorne held out his phone. On it were private stills of a mature woman, naked below her neck and unseen face. Olive knew it was his umpteenth squeeze since her mother's recent death. Alarmed, Lorne flicked to what he'd meant to reveal: two tickets to Fyfe Moreso's new concert.

"Tomorrow night," he said. "Take them. Otherwise, they'll go to waste."

Olive gasped, audibly. With his stubby fingers, Lorne sent the tickets to her phone. A lion's roar from her backpack meant they'd been received. Then her father lingered long enough in the space between her room and the hall, her world and his, to be acclaimed as a great guy before he left.

Olive felt her father had given her access to something wonderful of which he wasn't aware: her true growing self. That was worth a kiss, planted quickly and glancingly on his cheek, before she closed the door.

The next afternoon, Olive was let out of an unmarked, self-driving van, the windows obscured by black blinds. On a city sidewalk, her phone was confiscated, and she was frisked by a stocky uniformed woman. Then she was led to the side entrance of an arena and into an elevator which went deep, she felt, into the earth.

In a basement shower stall, Olive stripped and was bathed, doused, and swabbed for germs. While waiting for the results (negative, it turned out), she was given a verbal quiz by a recorded, disembodied voice. ("Where was Fyfe Moreso born?" "How old is he?" "How many siblings does he have?") Olive was versed enough in Moreso-abilia to know and say that "any answer is correct." She filled out a questionnaire to check the possibility of her committing violent and/or disruptive acts during the show, which she "aced," she was happy to learn. From there, she was allowed to take her seat in a huge, mostly deserted stadium.

Madison Square Garden only sporadically held entertainment and sports events now, doing quadruple duty as a homeless shelter, vaccination center, criminal-holding pen, and armory. Only a few rows, scattered at great distances, would be used for the show, due to the new Airborne Illness Index of Very, Very Bad (VVB). Olive was in the fifth row.

The other attendees were either lottery winners or as privileged and connected as she. Most of them (she counted sixteen) were women as young if not younger, with a few mothers and hostile fathers thrown in. Olive tried to temper her admittedly petty sense of jealousy toward these girls. She wished to have Fyfe to herself, even if in the near-distance, elevated on a stage. She wanted to think he'd be singing strictly for her.

The lights dimmed.

In the cavernous dark, Olive could hear not only her own halting breath but that of the other girls. Olive thought: they would all lose because she would win. She was a fair, perhaps excessively ethical person—her father thought so, anyway. Yet hidden in the great giant blind spot of MSG, in which she saw and heard no judgment, she was free to feel as competitive and heedless and carefree as she was growing to become.

Then one light drew Olive's attention elsewhere.

Fyfe Moreso was illuminated in the pin spot. As was his wont, he looked every which way and remained no way for long: young, old, short, tall, male, female, androgynous. His attire appeared to alter every second, as if projected upon him in old-fashioned slides: plaid shorts, clown shoes, purple afro wig, crew cut, tux, safari jacket, even no clothes at all (though his nudity was either an optical illusion or an expression of his audience's sublimated wish). Fyfe's singing voice hopped from high to low, bass to falsetto; then all ranges overlapped, as if a radio dial had been spun on a car ride back when one could still freely travel cross-country.

Olive wondered if this, too, was a hologram. Then she smelled Fyfe in the air, the breath from his mouth, the sweat from his pores and glands, his perfume and body odor, mouthwash, chicken tikka masala, and crotches of every kind.

Present in all his incarnations and under each accessory was Fyfe's strange, specific softness, which was a type of trademark. He was hairless, wan, and concave, so smooth he seemed translucent, like a wave you slipped and slid on to enter an ocean. His bare skin flowed like spit or semen or the tears one shed—Olive felt like shedding—when you saw him. The hanks of hair here and there, beneath his arms, between his legs, revealed for a second, or so she thought, in the strobe-like shifts of what she saw, were like waving grass under that ocean. All of it was why Olive adored him and her father and most men felt contempt.

As for his music—did it matter? Many thought it didn't, many adults, anyway, for whom Fyfe's head-bending blend of styles was nothing but noise: punk, which eased into oompah, before becoming big band, giving over to glam rock and German lieder, heading to a hoedown, and ending in Eine Kleine Nachtmusik. For his young fans, it was the aural approximation of the alterations going on inside them, the eons of emotions that existed and died off every day, the contradictory passions only their peers could appreciate (as it had once been for their parents, an idea against which they violently and incredulously fought).

Today, it was no different. Olive could not resist Fyfe's music, which was like the song of the siren in the story politicians forbade her to read in school. Circe, that was her name, the woman who seduced sailors to the bottom of the sea. Olive could not restrain her own flood of feelings as she heard him call to her. She shut her eyes to keep inside the tears she wished to expel as answer. When she opened them, she saw Fyfe Moreso as if through a wet and shredded curtain, as if she were actually underwater. She could not trust what she witnessed, could not believe that it was true.

Moreso *was* looking—singing—directly at her.

He had come to the lip of the stage to do it, and "lip" was a fitting phrase, for it was as if he was poised on that part of himself, pointing at her. Soon Fyfe extended a hand, the pale palm of which shone as brightly as a nuclear blast in the spotlight isolating it. He gazed at her with eyes blue, brown, green, and Rosemary's Baby-red, all at the same time.

Olive did not remember rising, though she obviously had. She was starting up onto the stage before being pulled up by Fyfe, who lifted her with almost no effort at all. Suddenly, she was opposite him, a few feet away.

Right to her, he sang all of his songs, which she knew by heart, becoming one long line of sound she opened her mouth to swallow, amazed and excited it was big enough to take in his whole catalogue. The entire time, he stared as if she were no stranger, he'd always known her and had been waiting for her to arrive.

It was now and here, without being touched by him or herself, in front of all those fans, the few, anyway, who had been allowed in, that Olive's public climax came. It was so powerful it killed the lights in Madison Square Garden and sent her falling, falling, down into the dark.

Olive was awakened by someone calling her name. She felt buried in an avalanche and her eyes shut by snow. When she forced them open, she saw a blurred version of her home, and only blinking like a flirtatious flapper made her bedroom recognizable. It was as starkly lit as the stage on which Fyfe Moreso had played. Had she even been there? Or had it been a dream? She realized she'd slept in her clothes, was even wearing shoes, one shoe, anyway, like some ecstatic Cinderella.

She heard her name again.

"Olive? Olive! Open the door!"

It was her father's voice and her father's knuckles knocking, as if he, too, were trapped. Olive lifted a body weighted down by stones and tried to walk on feet still asleep. She hit her door like a sea gull smashed against a windshield. She heard her father cry, "Hey!" and back off in the hall.

Opening the door, Olive found him flat against the opposite wall, where he had fled to safety.

"Good morning," she wheezed, not sure she could be heard.

"Late afternoon," Lorne said, peeling himself off the wallpaper and approaching.

Before Olive could thank him for the tickets, her father bellowed into her already aching ears…

"He said yes!"

"What? Who?"

"You know! That sickeningly soft little creep! He said he'll do the party!"

Shocked, Olive was able to understand he meant Fyfe. Yet her father seemed furious about it.

"But…isn't that good?" she asked.

"No! He said he'd do it for nothing! He said he'd pay *me*!"

Olive's father stared at her, assuming his insinuation was obvious. Yet it wasn't, for nothing was clear to Olive today. Lorne came closer and spoke softly, as if his next sentence shouldn't be shared in a shout by the civilized.

"He saw you at his show. He sang to you. I think we both know what he wants in return."

This time, her father shut the door, so loudly it obscured Olive's answer, which was a question.

"We do?"

Olive couldn't tell her father that he was wrong: Fyfe Moreso wasn't bartering for her, swapping for her sexual favors. She was thoughtful that Lorne had jumped to this conclusion, assumed everyone was as underhanded as he. He seemed to suffer turning Fyfe down, because being moral made him miserable. This gave Olive a new insight into her father, one that was not so nice.

Still, Olive couldn't tell Lorne he was wrong, because she didn't know what Fyfe actually wanted of her. She knew it was something different and deeper than what her dad (and, frankly, any father) would think. Yet that Fyfe seemed eager, even desperate, to participate in the party after seeing and singing to her, made Olive beside herself with happiness. It meant he might feel a fraction for her what she felt for him. Were his emotions as mysterious to him as hers were to herself? She considered this, saying little, as Lorne began to look for a star replacement, often mispronouncing the names of new and trending attractions.

Then, one night, Olive's phone roared.

She saw a logo on an incoming text. It was another, smaller hologram, a flickering oval that waxed and waned like the sun when clouds cover and uncover it, the kind credit cards used when people still carried and weren't covered by tattoos of them. It was the officially licensed logo for Fyfe Moreso and his music.

Soon the corporate ID faded and revealed behind it, as if rubbed out of steam on a mirror after a shower, was Fyfe Moreso's floating face.

Fyfe blinked and smiled in the small circle on the screen. Was it a pre-recorded replica of the real thing, Olive wondered, like the performance she had pressed against and kissed? Had this moment been made months ago and preserved for whoever wished to watch? Olive learned otherwise.

"Olive?" he said.

The singer appeared as a stable persona, not different singers every second; he was merely his own soft self. His eyes, only brilliant blue, held her, hypnotically.

"Yes?" Olive asked.

"Come see me," Fyfe said.

"Excuse me?"

"Your father won't let me sing for you. Even for free. Come see me. Please."

Fyfe's speaking voice was as smooth, clear, and leveled as his chest, arms and legs, as his un-bearded face.

His words were being improvised and addressed to her as they occurred to him.

"Where," Olive asked, "should I go?"

Fyfe told her. Before she could ask any question, he dissolved into bits and pieces like falling fireworks, as did his company logo. This left behind Olive's screensaver, another picture of Fyfe Moreso.

Fyfe had given her the location of his next show, unknown to anyone else: hackers worldwide always tried and failed to find them. It was in an unfree state requiring an adult from her free state to have a domestic passport. Olive had never filed for one.

She would go see Fyfe or die.

Interstate travel—especially from a free state to an unfree—was uncommon, and most events were attended virtually. Olive secretly transferred money from a passive trust fund account to an active one, swallowing the penalty she incurred as an acceptable punishment, the pain she had to endure to get pleasure or pain that was pleasure itself, like the electric shock kiss she fantasized getting from Fyfe's facsimile: all of this was still embryonic to her.

Olive went to find the place to get the passport. It was in a former church on a neglected side street of town, alongside once impressive and now abandoned and overgrown homes. Bags of garbage sat unattended on the curb, some being ripped and rifled through by rats and the homeless. Olive side-stepped hyperactive rodents and almost unconscious humans to get inside.

There was an old-fashioned feeling to the space, like perfunctory areas in public schools and housing projects where people had once been allowed to vote. In fact, the photo machine for Olive's ID was an actual ancient voting booth, a standing box fronted by a frayed curtain made of the cheapest cloth. Pews sat empty except for the occasional leaf or piece of plaster fallen from or through the ceiling in super storms.

"Can I help you?"

Olive turned. Hobbling toward her on a stiff left leg was a plumpish young man who had entered through an interior door, left open to reveal a staircase leading down. As he approached, Olive could see that his pants were baggy, slung almost to his buttocks, and the stained white T-shirt he wore had one obscenity professionally if crudely embossed with flames shooting out from every letter.

"Hey," Stark said, "look who's here."

Olive hadn't seen Starker Braun since high school. He had always been a bad penny, the son of a wealthy doctor whom it was said trafficked in foreign medicines unapproved in the U.S. Olive heard Stark had recently been injured in a robbery attempt at his estranged father's house, hence the bum leg. He had been released by police after his father refused to file a complaint, washing his hands of his son. Stark had been expelled from the local park where he'd been living after being shooed out by the homeless shelter. He had also, inexplicably, since their adolescence, loved Olive.

"I'm working here now," Stark said, as if Olive were about to ask. "Also living. For free. It's a sweet deal. I've got a nice bunk in the basement. When that gets too hard on the heinie, I can sack out on excelsior." Wood shavings, conceivably on the floor. "Soft! And speaking of soft..."

Now Stark openly ogled Olive. To distract, him, she pointed to the booth.

"Are you in charge of..."

"What? Oh. Yes."

"Well...shall we?"

"If I've got anything to say about it..." he answered, pruriently, "yeah!"

Through the booth's sheer curtain, Olive saw a tattered white background against which a person would pose. Stark was the photographer, she supposed, in addition to his chores as a custodian: he had stashed a basic broom and dustpan near the door after coming upstairs.

Walking was difficult for him, given his damaged leg, cut by the glass of his father's window. Still, she sensed this had nothing to do with why he was standing still.

"I won't do it," he said.

"Why not?"

"It won't do you justice."

"What won't?"

"The photo."

Olive didn't know what to reply. Suddenly, time seemed ticking away. She feared she wouldn't make Moreso's show, which was only hours from now. She felt impatient and anxious alone with him.

Stark moved toward her, not the booth. He stood so close Olive could smell the dust of his digs downstairs and the burned morning coffee still powdering his mouth. Unlike Moreso's aromas, Stark's made her feel sick, not excited. She sensed the possibility of being harmed by him, but this wasn't like the erotic idea of being burned by Fyfe. Olive was amazed by what a difference the other person in her dreams made. More of her ongoing education, she thought.

"I can do you…" he said.

"What?"

"Justice."

Speaking directly into her ear, Stark recited a monologue that was not what she had been expecting. Yes, he promised what acts he would perform with and on her. Yet it was whispered with what Stark intended as passion, warmth, and even love. Stark pledged to give Olive pleasure as she—no one—had ever known it. In its aftermath and her afterglow, her mouth still expelling breaths, her head lolling limply on her pillow, her hair curled and wet with sweat from her exertions and tears in her eyes squeezed out by desire and disbelief (his phrases), then and only then would he take her picture. It was both a proposal and an act of extortion, the only way, Olive guessed, Stark could get any woman to say yes; that's how readily he had always been rejected. Even with her inexperience, she knew she was about to become one more woman he would blame for his disastrous actions.

"Sorry," she said.

Olive fled, untangling herself in a sense from Stark, for he had spun a web of sticky words around her. She heard his voice echo in the empty structure, pigeons fluttering in the eaves or whatever they were called, perceiving the same threat. Stark yelled, "Olive!" then replaced her name with harsher, hateful words, stamping obscenities on her like the sort-of notary he was for a price she wouldn't pay.

Curled in a ball, Olive wept for hours behind the closed

door of her room. Missing a Fyfe Moreso show to which she had been specially invited for an unknown reason made her more miserable than any illness, even those for which there had been no vaccines and which she had simply survived by chance.

She staggered to her phone and again coaxed from it the moving image of Fyfe, as if summoning a ghost in a séance. She made so many Moresos she had soon amassed an airy army of them, his apparitions singing out of sync, then swarming around Olive in the small space.

Olive put them all on mute and pause. They stopped, waiting for her to allow them to live again, or whatever it was they had been doing.

One Fyfe Moreso still sang.

His tiny, tinny voice was coming from an open window on her phone. It was a brand-new song she didn't know by heart. Olive realized this rendition was not a reproduction but happening as she heard it, at the same time he was singing and introducing it to a giant, global audience. This was the concert Olive had been invited to attend. Because she hadn't come, Fyfe had made it available to her, free of charge, online.

The sun had long since set. Olive's phone was the only illumination in her room. It pulsed on its stand like an object unearthed on another planet in a sci-fi film, one which held either all the wisdom of the world or a murdering alien with twelve tiers of teeth. Olive sat, entranced, before it.

As she had at his actual show, Olive knew he sang to her alone. She memorized the new tune immediately.

Then, slowly, it changed. The tempo, lyrics, and arrangement began to go backwards, to retreat in time, to fade to fit into an earlier decade. Fyfe Moreso's music again entered Olive's mouth, this time leaping through electronic layers to sink into and separate her lips. Olive passed out or became unconscious while awake. Either way, she was traveling with him, into the past.

It was Columbus Day, 1944, a school holiday. Olive was celebrating something else. She was going downtown, as soon as she could wake up the young man beside her, Wilbur.

Olive gave him a little shove but he simply snuffed, sort of snored, and shifted in her narrow bed. His beefy arm was crushing her, and Olive wasn't strong enough to lift him or ease out from under him to escape. They'd both fallen asleep in their clothes—Wilbur hadn't even taken off his standard issue Army shoes—and Olive had barely slept at all, she'd been so excited.

"Wilbur?" she whispered. "Wilbur? Come on, I've got to go."

She pushed and pushed until, complaining, possibly in a dream, Wilbur rolled away. Olive took the opportunity to stand and start to change. Making sure the soldier still had his eyes shut, she stripped and yanked up her new pantie-girdle with the satin front panel before putting on her white dress with the bow tie at the throat, a tribute to Tony Cantare, since he always wore one. She secretly hoped—though she knew it was nuts—that Tony would see it from the stage.

Olive was brushing her hair in the mirror when, behind her, she saw Wilbur start to stir. He attempted to blink himself awake, still feeling the effects, she figured, of all those beers from last night, two bottles of which lay empty on her floor. As usual, her mother was sleeping it off, too, down the hall, after drinking something harder. She wouldn't have been awakened if a Nazi bomb dropped on their building. Otherwise, Mom might have belted her one if she caught Wilbur in her room, let alone her bed. Though, to be honest, she still thought they were kids and not twenty, Wilbur growing up across the street and all. Not that the two of them had actually *done* anything last night, not for lack of trying on Wilbur's part, now all hands and full of new "knowledge" since getting old enough to join the army. Olive was glad he'd soon be going back after his leave, which made her feel bad, because what if he got shipped overseas (and killed)? Anyway, she better get a move on if she was going to make it to the Paramount on time.

"Hey," Wilbur said, his voice garbled.

"What?"

"For a minute, I thought I was back at the base." He began to sit up then, wincing, remained flat. "Where are you going at six a.m., to the parade?"

"Maybe."

"My father's working it."

His dad was a cop. Olive's dad was dead, which was one reason her mother was a drunk.

"Never mind," she said. "It's where *you're* going. Home."

Wilbur groaned, and she couldn't tell if he were heartbroken, hungry, or just hungover. Even if she'd had half a crush on him once—when they were twelve!—those days were long gone. Olive was all Tony's now, though she wouldn't tell Wilbur.

It turned out she didn't have to.

"Oh," he said, suddenly. "I know!"

"What do you think you know?"

"Why you're all dolled up."

She'd been putting on lipstick while they were talking, she hadn't even been aware.

"To see that skinny bum, that…"

Wilbur used a few more choice ugly words to describe Tony, insults that made Olive doubly aware he was an adult now, or thought he was, anyway, in his new uniform, and no longer the boy next door.

"I notice *he's* not in uniform. Why is that?" he said.

"I told you, his inner ear."

"Yeah, right. Either he paid his way out or they're not taking his type..."

Standing up, Wilbur pursed his lips and bent his wrist, implying Tony was effeminate. He had been energized by anger, Olive thought, and by envy of Tony, but she couldn't say that. Then he used a few more words, including some she didn't know but the meaning of which was clear.

"I'm not sure why a girl would want a guy like that when she could have..."

And then he took tight hold of her hand, her wrist, and pulled her back onto the bed. This was no joke, since Olive had just gotten dressed, and Wilbur was already adding wrinkles to what she wore, his hands going everywhere as they had last night, as they did all day when she saw him now. She'd heard from a friend that Wilbur had been "active duty" since enlisting, which meant he'd slept with lots of girls, new slang she hadn't known until now. Well, maybe *they* liked being mauled, but he was hurting her and making it hard to get away.

"You've become such a dish," Wilbur murmured and sounded really excited. She could feel he was excited, too, against her leg, which only made it worse. What *wasn't* hard about him now?

"Knock it off. My mother's in the next room."

"She'll never know."

He made a drunken glug-glug-glug sound, not a nice way to talk about the woman who for years had welcomed him into her home whenever his parents had a fight, which was all the time.

"I said—stop!"

"Aw, nuts!"

With the greatest reluctance, Wilbur let her go. Then he went back to berating Tony, his small size, his wispy ways, his ridiculous voice, which he imitated cruelly, sounding more like a moose than the greatest singer of all time, Olive thought. She hated Wilbur now and, if she wasn't so worried that he'd get killed in the war, she would have told him so. She just said…

"Please…go away."

"Come to the parade. My dad will get us a good place."

Wilbur spoke almost sweetly and Olive was taken by his tone and almost tempted. But it was too late, she was in love with someone else. Besides, she soon learned Wilbur was being phony. He yelled at her, from the window of her room, as she emerged onto West Eighty-Seventh Street, not caring if her mother or their neighbors or everybody on Earth could hear…

"Go! Go to that…"

…and finishing with as filthy a collection of words as Olive had ever heard.

On the subway—of course—she was groped again. This time, it was by a coward who took his chance in the crowd at Seventy-Second, changing trains for the express. For the one long stop to Times Square, Olive stood with her back against the doors: at least look in my eyes when you do it, you crumbs, she thought.

It was all a blur after she got out: how did she even reach the Paramount on Forty-Third? She knew her plan had been brilliant: getting there so early, there was no crowd yet for the ten a.m. show. Her friend, Gina, was waiting beneath the larger-than-life Tony Cantare atop the marquee. She wore a bow tie, too, plus bobby sox, and had a picture of Tony pinned to her dress.

"This way," Gina said, very comically dramatic, curtsying, and pointed to the alley.

Gina's father was a janitor in the building across the alley, so she knew the ins and outs. There was an entrance to the Paramount's fire exit stairway, and through this door they went. Soon the two were inside the unoccupied theater, three hours early.

They had to hide in the ladies' room. It was cleaner than Olive's bathroom at home, because her mother was always too blind to clean up and not break her perfume bottles all the time. Gina had brought doughnuts, there was sink water to wash them down with, and the girls made sure to sing Tony's songs too quietly to be heard in the hall and enjoyed making echoes. When it was time, they sneaked in through the side door to the auditorium, which brought them right to the front row (Gina should have been an allied spy, she'd done the recon so well).

By now, the place was nuts. Years later, Olive learned there had been anywhere from 3600 to 5000 people, mostly young, largely female. The smell of sweat, cheap scent and—if Olive wasn't insane—pee was overpowering. The building seemed ready to levitate from the energy in it; each person anticipated an explosion and had lit her own fuse. To calm them down, the orchestra played the "Star Spangled Banner," encouraging patriotism, sobriety, and silence, but it stopped and started nothing. The lights began to dim before anyone was ready. There was no way to be; how could you be ready for your own adulthood, your aging, your own death? They all seemed instants away.

The orchestra struck up Tony's latest hit, "(I Was) Too Happy to Dream." Cries of excitement were so loud they drowned out the music, and only the curtains parting—slowly, teasingly, like somebody's lips—informed Olive that something was about to change. Then there he was, like the tongue from between the teeth, all twenty years, five foot seven and 120 pounds of Tony Cantare. He was dressed in brown slacks, a brown and yellow plaid jacket, flaming orange sweater and bow tie, and a white shirt with points "like two pieces of pie," the *Daily News* would say later, but more like the flowing robes of the last deity you saw before you were born, deflowered, and died. He didn't bless anyone, he only smiled, shyly, as if he'd had nothing to do with being anointed, it had just happened to him. He opened his mouth to sing in a voice too full of feeling to be found in his skinny frame: it, too, had been placed there without his understanding how. This didn't silence the crowd; if anything, it screamed louder with each expression of his breath, every tender line and lyric of "(I Was) Too Happy to Dream," "I Married the Moon (and the Stars)," and "I'll Win (the War) for You."

During the show, like any decent god, sometimes Tony grew weary of being worshipped. He tried to teach them all to "listen to better songs." He performed pieces where the music was classical but the words were about the war, first love, or getting your house ready for

Christmas. He hoped they'd see his new movie, *Faster and Faster*, which was the sequel to *Get Going*, his last hit, and the three others to follow, *Quick Step*, *First One In*, and *Straight Up Joe*, his first drama, he said, though there was singing in it, too. It didn't matter what he said or sang, the reaction was always the same—shrieks, laughs, and "We love you Tonys"—the way thunder always follows lightning, no matter how much or little it had lit up anything.

At last, seeming exhausted, Tony blew kisses with both hands and backed off the stage. The curtain covered him again, not like lips, Olive thought, more like giant eyelashes falling over his bewitching blue eyes, now grown so great in the sky they would watch over everyone going out and make sure they got home safe.

Olive didn't go home, no matter how much Gina begged her to. Gina said she had homework: even if it was a holiday, there was still school tomorrow. Plus, you had to pay to see the next show, and it wasn't fair to freeload. Gina was better than Olive; both had been good girls but Olive was now something else, not naughty, not so *normal*, but whatever she had become because she was convinced Tony had been singing to her alone the whole time. It wasn't her imagination, it was her secret, and she couldn't say it out loud.

By herself, Olive hid in the ladies' room again, waiting for Tony to reappear. The next show was at two. By now, she was so hungry she was lightheaded. Unlike people whom not eating made nasty, she became more benign, lenient, and loving, as if Tony—with his beneficent attention—had blessed her and left her accepting of everything. She made sure to take the same seat for the second show and sat next to a new girl this time. Feeling allied to everyone on Earth, Olive said she'd seen the show and she, the girl, was in for something "swell."

By now, fifty ushers had been added but, whether old or new, their uniforms and ties had been torn, and they looked weary and afraid. The bodies of girls who had either fainted or pretended to faint spotted the aisles.

When Tony came out, he was dressed differently but Olive was too busy staring at his lips to notice. The noise that greeted him was cacophonous yet seemed to cut out, quickly, and there was silence instead as he opened his mouth for Olive only, his Adam's Apple quivering and pulsing, shrinking and extending. When so many of his silent songs were over, Tony's voice became audible to her again, as if she alone were touching and turning up the knob of his volume. Staring right at Olive, he said…

"You've been here all day. Isn't your family concerned or aren't you hungry?"

The audience laughed like crazy and clapped and called out answers Olive couldn't comprehend. She was too busy mouthing "yes" to him, meaning, yes, she was hungry, but also everything else that "yes" could mean. And then a guy in a chef's outfit came out from the wings to cheers from the crowd, carrying a tray of milk and sandwiches. Olive realized this was both a pre-arranged comedy "bit" and a cover for what he really wanted to do.

Tony reached out his hand and nodded to encourage Olive to come up. Soon a stagehand was helping her to hoots, whistles, and a few envious boos, and Olive ascended a small flight of stairs. Then she was opposite Tony, not even an arm's length away. She could see how wet and shiny was his face and smell his cologne, which was identical to her own fragrance. In front of everyone, she swallowed hard ham he handed her splattered with mayonnaise and cushioned by soft white bread, which was glided down her throat by milk. Tony stood near her, nodding encouragement again. Right before she finished, he whispered, too softly for anyone but her to hear…

"Save me."

Like so many aspects of this experience, the next few minutes were a mirage to Olive. Somehow, she ended up backstage as the curtain came down, the applause and acclaim fading into the past as Tony and she fled down a hall, just the two of them. They must have entered an elevator, for how else could they have gotten where they ended up? A heavyset middle-aged man operated the car, a cigar sticking from his mouth, either amused or annoyed by his passengers. After Tony pushed a bill into the guy's front shirt pocket as they came to a stop, two, three or four flights in the air, the guy called Tony "champ" to thank him, and "chump" behind his back, Olive was almost sure. Then they were in some suite that served as his apartment during his appearances, looking down on the street. Below, it looked like a political rally in the unfree countries they were fighting, everyone with no choice but to attend, that's how packed with people Times Square was.

"Jeez," Tony said, softly, to himself after he lifted the blind, as if he were only an observer and not the object of all this attention. "Will you look at that."

He seemed very young to Olive then, younger than he was, which was her own age, so younger than her. He seemed slighter, too, his body breakable or the pieces merely malleable, like a doll for which she was too old yet loved more and more at every age. She could not have loved him more than at that moment.

Then Tony turned from the window. With one delicate yet definitive yank, he undid his bow tie. The two sides fell and hung limply at equal lengths like paper puppet legs. With a thumb, he pushed open the button underneath it, parting the sides of his shirt at the top and revealing an inch of skin at the base of his throat, which was olive-colored—olive, Olive thought, like her. Tony seemed to have done it to free himself not just physically but for something he needed to say.

"I've been cursed," he said, his voice hoarse from so much singing or the sheer strain of carrying this confidence inside for so long.

"You *have*?" Was being a star such a burden? That's what the fan magazines said, though even she knew it was only to appease ordinary people like her and make them feel okay with their lousy lives.

"Yes." His voice cracked like an ice cube split in his young man's mouth.

"Cursed to do what?"

"This. Forever."

"Sing?"

"Yes. And be alone."

Olive nodded, startled by the information. It was as if someone had said, "Here's the thing you spend all day and night desiring. Only I know what it is, and you can have it."

Yet it wasn't that simple and Tony didn't stop there.

In a speaking voice just as mellow and tender as the one he used to sing—though filled with more yearning and desperation, as if he were dredging something up from the depths of himself and letting it spill from his mouth—he told Olive his tale of woe.

Tony had been a star many times, under different names, years and years before, over centuries, in other ages. He had never been able to cease, been sentenced to drift and never die. It wasn't his idea, it had been imposed on him by the devil. The only thing that could stop him was the love of a loyal woman, and he'd always been betrayed. Tony more than implied that he'd been saving himself for whoever she was. Despite the avidity and availability of his female fans, he'd never known anyone intimately. Olive intuited that Tony always started over in this way each time he existed, and that these betrayals came after he had lost his innocence. She wasn't sure, but it made sense. Anyway, he was staring at her, for she was the one for whom he'd been waiting.

Olive undid her own bow tie, though less adroitly than had he, who was more used to wearing one: she had to tug it a few extra times. So that there would be no mystery as to what she wanted—that she would be his and his alone—and that she had just as little idea of what she was doing in this area as he, she gave a shrug of *here goes*. Then she unbuttoned the buttons below her collar and opened her dress for him, to say, *Let's see how we do*.

And before either one knew it, her chemise and bra were ringed and flapped over at her waist, and she was feeding herself to him, her breasts in his mouth, a man's mouth for the first time, her nipples rolled so hard and red they looked like the cherry ices she would suck herself before a ball game, above and beneath his teeth.

"You really are so pretty," Tony said, nearly on his knees, moaning in that famous voice and Olive joining in, unable to keep still.

Then she was pulling his belt this way and that until she opened his impeccably pleated pants and revealed his silk drawers, before she took them down. Then all hell broke loose, his penis and pubic hair destroying his elegant ensemble with animal disarray, ruining everything with how ready he was and how big was his erection. It was the first one she'd ever seen and it was Tony's, too, not Wilbur's or someone's on a subway car or whoever's she'd felt without wanting to, as real and as secret as what he'd said about himself.

Amazed, Olive couldn't keep away from it. Just as she took him in her hand, Tony whispered, "Oh no," and quickly moved her to the side, the way a photographer might move a fan to get a better angle, except Tony did it considerately, so as not to ruin the white dress Olive had to wear home.

Afterward, Tony looked older, Olive thought. But how was someone as ancient as he supposed to look? In any case, he seemed calmer. Would this have a negative impact on his four o'clock show, since intensity and suppressed hysteria were his stock in trade? Olive wouldn't know. She said that her mother was expecting her at home, which wasn't true—her mother had probably only just woken up—but maybe she wished it was.

Tony felt sure they would see each other again; that was the calm part, she concluded. He gave her his private number and she gave him hers, though it was already available to anyone. That night, she thought, as the song said, they would both be too happy to dream.

Tony insisted that his private bodyguard get her through the mob outside. He'd heard that dozens of cops had been diverted from their duties at the Columbus Day Parade. (Like Wilbur's father? she wondered.)

"Thanks," she said, for this made her feel safe.

"I'll see you soon," he said.

"You know where I'll be," she said.

Tony took her hand and placed it on the silken place over his heart, as if this was where she meant. Olive stepped forward and kissed that space on his shirt. Then she pulled back, panicked to find that she'd left a red lipstick outline there.

"You'll change?" she asked, to make sure.

Tony nodded. He meant that, knowing her, he already had.

A week later, Olive learned what he was doing from a newspaper. She'd been waiting for Tony to get in touch; she knew he was on the West Coast, shooting scenes for his new movie, *Go Down Joe*, a sequel to *Straight Up Joe*. Olive read in the columns that, to the shock of show business, he was considering retirement: "Songbird Tony Tuckered Out! Thrush to Rest His Voice for Good?" This gave her hope about herself and him.

Olive had been avoiding Wilbur, whose leave ended soon. Yet, as a certain boxer said, she could run but she couldn't hide.

"Where you been?" the soldier asked in her doorway one night, after her mother had gone to bed.

"Nowhere." Olive could already smell the beer on him, and it wasn't even eight.

"How was the show?"

"What show?"

"You know. On Columbus Day. Starring that…" And Wilbur called Tony the same names as before, this time preceded by even more obscenities.

Olive shrugged, to suggest the show had been whatever he wanted it to be. Wilbur was still on her threshold; she hadn't asked him in, and he hadn't taken the hint.

"He's even shorter than I thought," he said. "I mean, in person."

As Olive looked at him with curiosity, Wilbur took the opportunity to enter.

"What do you mean?" she asked.

"You got anything cold to drink?" He spoke as if ordering in a noisy bar.

"Shh." She nodded at the bedroom.

Wilbur made a face that meant, *Quit pulling my leg, the old lady's dead to the world.* She didn't answer his question and asked her own instead.

"What do you mean, 'in person'?"

She had to follow Wilbur to find out, for he was headed to the kitchen. There he opened the icebox, but there was no beer, because her mother drank booze, which was rationed, and they'd run out. Wilbur shut the cooler door, disappointed.

"It means I saw him," he said.

He combed through the cupboards, where he found Saltines and spoke through them as he ate two at a time.

"Where?" Olive asked.

"At the Paramount, where else? As he was leaving. My pop was moved over from the parade. He called me and said come down. What a gas. One wolfess after another clutching the poor little guy. As I said, he was small…" He placed his hand only a few inches from the floor, as a gag. "Dad and the other cops kept him from being trampled to death."

"Where were *you*?"

Wilbur sprayed crumbs with the b's in the next sentence. "By the boy's side. Dad can charm the birds off the trees. He said, 'Meet my son.' Tony was friendly enough, I guess, for a loser. I felt a little sorry for the fella, trapped by all those dolls and dillies. Admittedly, so many were dogs or just kids. I opened my wallet and showed him a picture of *my* girl. 'Take that, Tony! No bobbysoxers for a soldier.' You know? 'I got a grown gal.'"

"You have a girlfriend?" Olive just blurted it out, not with jealousy, for she didn't feel any, but the way you insult a sibling.

"See for yourself."

Cracker flakes falling from his fingers, Wilbur went into his uniform pocket and produced a wallet. Carefully, as if fishing it from fluid in a darkroom, he retrieved a snapshot, turned it around, and showed her.

Olive saw herself in black-and-white. In front of her

stoop, she was pulling a goofy glamor girl pose, hand behind head, one foot flung up behind. She had done it as a favor for Wilbur, right before he got inducted.

Olive exclaimed—she wasn't sure what, a mix of amazement, regret, and rage. She felt sorry for Wilbur, shame if she'd led him on, and grief that he'd never give up on getting her. Mostly, though, she was furious at him and afraid. Wilbur might have ruined it with Tony. He'd fear he'd lost the one loyal woman who could lift the curse.

"Well, what did *he* say?" she asked, desperately.

"It was funny." Wilbur was perplexed. "Little Tony seemed upset. Then angry. Then frightened."

Olive barely remembered throwing Wilbur out, how she'd literally pushed him down the hall to the front door, crying, the way you would a car up a hill after it had gone dead. Wilbur had laughed but she sensed he was heartbroken she hadn't been thrilled he'd shown Tony the photo and cared more about the guy to whom she'd shown it. Wilbur castigated Tony again in the ugliest and most adolescent ways, loud enough to wake up Olive's mother, which, of course, he didn't do.

Over and over, Olive tried to reach Tony but got no reply. The last time she called, she was told by an operator his personal number had been changed, and the new one was unavailable.

Weeks later, she read that, after playing a sold-out show in Boston, Tony had lingered outside the theater long after the crowd went home. Apparently intoxicated, bellowing about "betrayal," he picked a fight with a local gang of toughs loitering on a corner, and got stomped so hard he had to be hospitalized.

This was the last Olive knew of Tony Cantare in the past. She never learned how or if Wilbur came home from the war. The music of the period was pushed out of Tony's mouth and sucked back into Fyfe Moreso's on the phone in her room, where she still sat. Then the style of the sound started shifting to another time's, turning electric in Olive's brain.

Now it was May, 1974. It had been more than luck, that's what Olive's teacher told her. It was the quality of her writing, the acuity of her thoughts. She knew that Miss Aker was rarely effusive—a word Olive had learned in her class—or falsely complimentary to kids *and* that Olive herself was often self-deprecating (another Aker-taught expression). So, she tried to accept the praise. After all, Olive had won the high school essay contest, been one of only three who had won on the entire length of Long Island, a large span of land near New York City. They'd been chosen to meet the essay subject, Baird Melody, the biggest pop idol since Tony Cantare, the biggest teen superstar of the nineteen-seventies.

Of the seventies *so far*. There Olive went again, finding fault with everything. Stay put in the positive, she secretly pledged: that's what Baird Melody would do. He was so upbeat and passionate in every song he sang.

Some said Olive was too old to idolize Baird. As a senior, now eighteen, she was the eldest of the three winners, the other girls fifteen and sixteen. Yet hadn't Miss Aker said that was the reason she *had* won, her essay was the most mature? Even the title, "Why I Hate Baird Melody," was a clever twist on the assignment, which was to explain, "Why I *Love* Baird Melody." Olive had turned it on its head to say that she *hated* the singer because he made her see how unexciting everything else was in her own life. It got your attention and made the essay more effective. Only a girl now grown up could have done that, said Miss Aker.

Of course, what did Miss Aker know? Olive thought. The teacher wasn't that old herself. She looked weirdly young in fact, especially to her male students, even sometimes wore an Indian bandanna around her stunning red hair, a mini-skirt and love beads. (Did she sometimes go braless too? Some of the girls were bitterly convinced of it.) No, Olive was determined to be positive. Maybe, being young, Miss Aker felt closer to Olive and her judgment about the essay was more credible. Right?

Olive was aware that her mind was racing, that she was trying to keep herself calm. She was sitting on a couch in a hotel room with the other girls, both coincidentally named Kathy, waiting for Baird Melody to show up (he was a half hour late). She couldn't do what those girls were doing, giggling and jabbering to each other. The two had been strangers until today; they came from towns miles apart on Long Island, yet had been immediately allied by their ages. This set them apart from Olive, who was so much older. Olive had to simply stay silent and feel utterly alienated and alone, almost panicked by how little anyone understood her, besides Baird Melody.

Then the door opened. A bald, middle-aged man appeared, who one of the Kathies whispered, authoritatively, was "a *publicist.*" He was followed immediately by Baird himself. He had given no one time to prepare, emotionally or any other way—Olive could only run a fast hand through her hair.

Olive thought Baird looked younger and older in person, if that was possible. His adult woman's rollercoaster-curled hair fell lankly past kid-sized shoulders; his un-muscled chest and gut were covered by a grown man's collarless disco shirt, and his narrow torso jammed into fashionable floppy elephant bells. His infant-blue eyes were cupped by black rings, and his thick, permanently puckered lips had no beard above or below them, like when you shook the shavings from an etch-a-sketch face. All of this made Olive adore him definitively and forever.

Despite obvious fatigue, Baird managed to lift those heavy lips into a boyish and apologetic smile and whisper…

"Sorry I'm late, girls. I just got in from the coast."

The two Kathies giggled, unable to answer, incapacitated by excitement, their braces seeming to gleam in the glow cast by Baird (Olive's own ornate dental ware had been dismantled three years ago). Before they became too embarrassing, Olive took it upon her more adult self to say, with a smile…

"That's okay. You're forgiven."

Did she just imagine that he stopped and looked at her longer than he had the other two? Had he seemed to even *recognize* her? Or was Olive merely being the idiot she always was? Whatever had just happened, Baird glanced at his publicist pal, seemed to snap to and remember to say…

"I'm going to love reading your essays."

He hadn't read them! Olive felt a dizzying sense of disappointment. She'd secretly suspected he'd single hers out for special praise, which he would communicate to her in a kind of code in order not to break the others' hearts. Of course, that never would have happened, only an imbecile would believe that, she knew it now. The others laughed even longer and shriller at this, and Olive felt like slapping them both until they cried.

Then Baird took a seat opposite, his pal hovering helpfully nearby. In a small voice—weakened by care? anxiety? jet lag?—he began to beseech them to take care as they moved through life.

"Please watch out for drugs, girls," Baird said. "And drinking. And fake friends. And don't make too much money, only enough."

He spoke by rote, as if this speech were well-rehearsed, even pre-recorded. All the while, was he staring only at Olive again? She dared to believe it was true.

"Now," he said, "I've told *you* something. It's your turn. What would you like to ask *me*?"

For the other girls, the two twits, it didn't matter what Baird had said. Yes, they progressed from laughing to actually using words; that was something, Olive thought. Yet all they wondered, breathlessly, was: What was (their favorite female TV star) really like? How many cars did Baird have? Did he think he'd ever get married? What was (their favorite male TV star) really like? They didn't address his deep concerns at all. Olive was about to break in and do so herself, when, suddenly, it was too late. What a dummy she had been for waiting!

"Okay, gals," the publicist said. "Baird's a tired cowboy. I hope you appreciate all he's done for you today, coming here."

The two Kathies applauded and madly nodded, their heads bobbing as if they were being back-slapped. All they could cough up was…

"Thanks, Baird! Great to meet you, Baird! Bye, Baird!"

"Bye, Kathies."

Impressively, Baird had remembered their names, Olive thought. She was preparing to excuse his not acknowledging *her* because she'd behaved like such a loser. Then he stopped at the door, stared right at her, and winked.

"You, too, Olive. Thanks for being so forgiving."

Olive was frozen by how much electricity Baird generated in her with the single utterance. Her spoken name sparked inside her like a blaze that would set the whole hotel, all of Long Island, on fire. She barely perceived the envelopes placed in each girl's palm by the publicist, after Baird left. The squeal of the others told her it held a ticket to the singer's concert on Long Island Saturday night.

After the three had been escorted into an elevator and out of the hotel, Olive realized her own envelope had an extra note inside, written by hand. It asked her to please meet Baird alone after the show. It ended with his autograph and the words, *Save me.*

Later, in her bedroom, Olive ran her fingers across the signature as if across Baird's lips. She was surrounded by pictures of him on music magazine covers, album sleeves, board game boxes. In the corner, a pile of TV Guides rose like a tiny tower built in tribute to Baird. His top-rated sitcom, *The Note House*, was on the front of every one, setting a record for how many times a show had been accorded the honor.

On the show, Baird played the oldest child in a rock and roll family act. His younger sister, Lulu, was a lovable tween know-it-all and the baby, a ten-year-old boy named Rusty, an adorable scamp. Their beautiful widowed mother played the tambourine in the group, and her boyfriend was their (kid-and-rock-and-roll-hating) agent, who was all bark and no bite.

Teenagers Olive's age disdained the show as embarrassing and for babies. While it had made him famous, Baird himself was eager to move on: his concert tour, including the appearance on Long Island, was an attempt to broaden his image and audience. Olive respected his wishes yet she'd secretly seen every *Note House* episode many times and would watch one more rerun this afternoon; she kept glancing at her Baird Melody clock to make sure she didn't miss it.

While she waited, she listened to forty-five after forty-five of Baird's biggest hits: "I Love a Love I Love," the biggest-selling song of 1972, despite its dismissal as "bubblegum junk" by music critics…"Summer Bummer," a comic number about a failed sleepaway camp romance, mocked by critics as "ridiculously" using a drug reference in a "completely failed" attempt to seem hip…and "Don't Dodge Our Love," the lyrics of which critics said were a "woefully dumb" way to allude to the Vietnam War.

When she looked up, Olive saw that the clock's second hand had shifted past Baird's bare shoulder. The episode had ended. Now Olive was going to be late for something else.

Even though she had a learner's permit, Olive raced across town on her bike, since her parents had taken both cars to work. She rode to a side street off the main drag, where the Village School was located. This was a new alternative to Olive's high school, a place established to placate activists who decried current curricula and methods of teaching as irrelevant to today's youth. Since students could choose their own courses and hours of attendance at Village, the class to which Olive pedaled had just let out, at five p.m. Outside the vine-covered structure, part of a rich family's estate donated for this "important purpose," as they put it, she saw Dooley waiting.

"Where you been?" he asked.

Dooley Kale was Olive's boyfriend, though he deplored definitive and bourgeois titles, preferring to keep things between them fluid and flexible. He came from a privileged background yet dressed in a dungaree shirt and dusty jeans decaled with peace signs. His chiseled face was hidden beneath a beard impressive for the twelfth grade.

"I had to run an errand for my mother," Olive lied.

Dooley shook his head, both sympathetic and disapproving. "Tote that barge," he said.

Olive couldn't tell him the truth, since Dooley had only contempt for Baird Melody and his music. She had intended to remove all Baird paraphernalia from her room after Dooley began pressuring her to let him come over, but she hadn't gotten around to it. Olive hadn't told him about the essay contest, either. She was glad Dooley had left the main high school for Village and hadn't heard about it.

"Can we *finally* go to your house?" Dooley asked, as Olive walked her bike beside him on a back road.

"My parents are still having the place painted." Olive had introduced this lie at some point, and would deal later with the fact that the house hadn't been painted, if he ever saw it.

"Okay," Dooley said, with displeasure. "I guess let's go to my house again."

Olive suspected that Dooley disliked running into his parents with her, since she was from the "wrong side of the tracks," the more middle-class part of town. She noticed he always brought her in through a back kitchen door his housekeeper used to take out trash.

"Sure you don't want?" Dooley asked, after he lit up a joint. He knew better and had only asked to needle her. Olive shook her head and shrugged.

"Suit yourself," he said. "You can watch out for the fuzz."

Dooley said this as a joke yet Olive was nervous they might be arrested, and any siren, no matter how far away, put her on edge. Her family, after all, wasn't connected enough to intimidate the cops, as was Dooley's.

"Here we go," Dooley said, as they reached the back kitchen door. He had Olive put her bike in the "mud room" area of a hallway she assumed his parents rarely visited.

Behind the closed door of Dooley's room, as usual, they fooled around on his bed beneath a Steely Dan poster Scotch-taped to the wall. Also as usual, she gave him a hand job to keep him from pressuring her to go all the way, which she had never done, not with anyone. After he finished, Olive wondered if what other girls said was true, that Dooley had had a "thing" with Miss Aker last year when he was in her class. This was why his parents had enrolled him in Village, to separate them. Dooley did seem strangely sophisticated about sex, she thought, about intercourse, especially. Anyway, Olive hadn't asked him about it and didn't think she ever would.

"What are you doing Saturday night?" he asked. "Some kids from Village are throwing a party."

The question caught Olive off guard, and she had no excuse at the ready. Saturday was, of course, the night of Baird's concert.

"My folks are having relatives over," she blurted out, perhaps reflexively referring to something that—when it actually occurred—she didn't enjoy, so sounding angry and sorry about it would seem real.

"And you have to be there?" he asked.

"Yes." Olive shook her head at the injustice. "They said I have no choice. The bastards."

Dooley fell silent as he finished buttoning his fly. Then he stopped in mid-hand-brushing of his lengthy hair.

"You *sure* you're not going to the Coliseum?"

This was the big outdoor stadium farther out on Long Island where Baird would be performing. Olive felt her face go red and then white; she swore she could sense the shift on her skin, like a strobe light in a movie drug scene. She turned away from Dooley, hoping her face would stop or at least settle on a shade. Suddenly, she realized telling the truth would be easier than inventing another lie. Meeting Baird had been the reason: he'd inspired her to be a better person. Still, she proceeded gingerly.

"What if I were?" she asked, as if curious.

Dooley took this as an admission of guilt. He barked a laugh that Olive thought defined the word *hollow* and shouted…

"Ho ho!"

…like a British TV detective finding a clue. Then he went into a familiar rant about Baird's shallow establishment sound, which he imitated by strumming an imaginary guitar with a conspicuously limp wrist. And this led him into a long monologue about Baird's missing manhood, which he said was proven by his sometimes singing in a falsetto. Dooley ended with what he considered his most cutting criticism…

"He even went to Vietnam with Bob Hope!"

At first, as she usually did, Olive received his screed in silence. Then she felt freed by having been at least a little honest with him. Her post-show invitation by Baird was the armor she wore to engage him.

Olive started her own—shakier—spewing of words at Dooley. She revealed she'd won the essay contest, back-tracked to tell him there'd *been* an essay contest and she had won…she now knew Baird Melody the man, and not only was she going to see his show but meet him *after*, that's how well she knew him…and not only did she love Baird's songs but she loved his sitcom too. What did he think about *that*?

Before Dooley could reply, Olive fled, without looking back, as if not to see the carnage caused by the tear gas and napalm she had just launched, that's how incendiary she felt her words had been. As she ran down one hallway after another, looking for her bike in the big, empty house, she heard Dooley yell, "Baird only wants to ball you, you're a little idiot who doesn't understand men," and, "Come back, Olive, I love you!"

At last, riding away, free to feel facetious, Olive wondered how Baird could both have sex with her *and* be castrated…whether Dooley was secretly railing about her refusal to sleep with him and hollering from hurt feelings about it ...and if Dooley might be right about her, after all, which suddenly seemed the most likely thing in the world and exactly what she deserved, stupid fool that she was.

Built on abandoned farmland, the Coliseum had a crude, makeshift quality, as if it were an old-fashioned revival tent show, uncovered to the elements. On Saturday, Olive was seated by Security beside the Kathies in the front row. Like the others, it was a removable set of seats that swayed disturbingly beneath the weight of the wiggling and squirming girls upon it. And it was almost all girls as far as Olive could see, when—poked by her neighbors—she turned to check the place out.

The first chord of the "Note House" theme song was struck by a pianist onstage who fronted a drummer, guitarist, and backup singers. Tall stalks of free-standing lights on each side were snapped off except for those that dazzlingly illuminated the stage.

To ear-splitting screams and applause, Baird bounded on. The logy character from the hotel room had been replaced by a spangly and hyper entertainer, decked out in tight flowered overalls over a scooped-neck T-shirt and diamond-studded, high-heeled boots. The music shifted into "I Love a Love I Love," Baird's biggest hit, which he proceeded to sing to—though not to be heard by—the cacophonous crowd. Baird punctuated his amped-up performance with karate kicks and fingers supposedly pointed at certain girls in the seats, though not at Olive, who told herself she was now too special to be falsely singled out.

Baird was panting when he finished this first song to thunderous applause, sweat sliding off him like grease in the temperate air. He watched impassively as a girl was pulled by Security from the stage, where she had crawled and was sliding on her stomach to reach him. Another girl, unconscious and faced upwards, was being carried by two men up the aisle, like a human sacrifice to him. Music awkwardly underscored these events as, in a weary voice, Baird began to beg…

"Please…please…move back. Or I can't continue and sing for you. The stage will collapse."

In fact, Olive had begun to hear creaking from the platform before and above her. As if he sensed his time running out, Baird swiftly segued into a darker mode. He aggressively led the musicians in a hard rock and roll song not heard on any of his albums. He belted out this number, which had something to do with the Delta and a Delta Lady; Olive could hardly hear it above the bellowing and heaving of the spectators. Then Baird began to growl in a lower, off-key register, vulgar and vulpine, turning his back to vigorously shake his small behind before swiveling back to thrust his even more compact crotch at the crowd, greeted by howls and high-pitched cries the more violently and contemptuously he came at them. At last, he trembled in place like a stripper, or so Olive imagined, as if trying to shake free sequins or some other accoutrement and leave himself nude. Far from sitting back and being seduced, the girls surged forward as one, to swarm over and smother him. Olive heard the stage moan more in misery.

Exhausted by this exposure of himself, Baird feebly shooed the pianist away from his perch at the instrument and sank upon the stool himself. He began to noodle on the keys, emitting a soft, lulling, off-key croon. His sounds steadily became words, only some of which were audible above the din of his devotees. Talk-singing, Baird lamented his position as "a puppet on a string," doing others' bidding. Soon the English words morphed into mournful French, and Baird became a pathetic "poupee." He ended the song in eerie quietude, tapping one lonely white key, as if knocking on the door to a deserted room. His followers had no clue, for they had been cawing and bleating all along.

"Please! Girls!"

This wasn't Baird but a bearded, paunchy stage manager, who had rushed on as Baird was being hustled off.

"You're all gorgeous! You're all beautiful! But we got to stop the show because you won't move back! The stage is collapsing!"

All lights splashed on. As orderly as if they were entranced, the enormous crowd began to exit, behind and around Olive. There were screams and laughter, and items as varied as flowers, photographs, lingerie, and rosary beads were left or lobbed onstage, volunteered or simply voided from his fans. As the singers and musicians escaped, the wooden flats beneath their feet grew unstable and wavy, like an ocean in which the possessions of the audience were being swallowed.

"This way."

Olive felt herself being pulled away from the Kathies by two security officers on either side. They guided her in and out of the exiting audience, elbowing as many people as needed to clear her path. They reached the aisle, then what looked like a one-lane road mowed from the field that led out of the arena. There they were joined by a thin woman in a simple sack dress and an old-school plastic rain bonnet on her blond hair.

"This way, Olive."

By now, they were far from the lights of the Coliseum, on a suburban side street lit only by the windows of distant homes and the headlights of a white Toyota, parked nearby. Its trunk was popped, the woman's bonnet removed and, with it, the blond wig. Without looking Olive's way, still in the dress, Baird bent to fit into the boot and curl up as the lid was dropped over him.

"This way."

The guards in back, Olive rode up front beside a young driver in a three-piece suit, sneakers on his feet a disobedient touch. They left one state and entered another, pulling at last into a Jolly Roger motel off the highway. It was a no-frills affair, neon bulbs in the images of a pirate and his parrot blown out above the revolving sign of the place's name.

Olive was escorted inside while, to her rear, Baird was freed from the bowels of the car. She glanced back to see the fringe pantlegs of Baird's overalls as he straightened his dress disguise down over them.

Accompanied by a silent, standing bodyguard, Olive waited in the small motel room, sparely decorated with a maritime theme. As Baird used the shower, his shift and wig lay on the bed beside her chair, waves and sailboats on the slipcover making them look like the remains of a drowned woman washed up on shore. After a brutally long wait, during which Olive yearned to yet could not use the bathroom to pee, Baird emerged.

He wore only a kimono. His wet hair was combed directly and elegantly back and his eyes were brighter than they had been all evening. He seemed psyched to have survived the same shipwreck.

Olive bolted past him to the john. She closed the door and was surrounded by Baird's steam, the smells of his sweat and hot cologne like soft whispers in her mouth. Long and short hairs from his head and genitals were Morse Code in the tub, the message too odd for her to understand. The toilet seat was slick with Baird when she sat on it.

Olive came out to find Baird by himself, no bodyguard in sight. Through the rusty blind, she saw the security detail now standing sentry in the parking lot. For a second, she was uneasy being alone with him. Yet the star sat on the bed with his nearly hairless legs tightly crossed, his arms protectively wrapped around himself, appearing more wary of her than she of him. His female garb lay inches away, at the ready, in case he needed it.

"Take a seat," he said, hoarsely, his voice hurt by the concert. Then he must have heard his preemptory tone. "Please."

After she was opposite him, not making eye contact, only seeking, as actors say, the middle distance above her head, Baird proceeded to recite a monologue. He revealed how little money he had made at the start of his sitcom, six hundred bucks a show, and nada from books and games. Performing live, on the other hand, was fifty G a pop, the reason he kept doing it, even after his agent had the network over a barrel because he was the breakout star, when he renegotiated the terms.

At first, Baird got off on the energy of the crowds and the pure rock and roll. This was the life! Now he was exhausted by them. He was a prisoner—look at this piece of shit place! The girls exhausted him offstage too. All the groupies were the same—they all wanted Baird Noteman, his character from the sitcom, not the real him. He made them pay for it in bed, those pigs, made them do anything he wanted, bark like a dog, play choo-choo train. They had no self-respect, anyway. He wanted to stop, wanted a change, a life, to be an actual artist, to have someone to love. He wanted…

Baird suddenly looked at Olive, for she was the end of the sentence. He blinked over and over, as if to be assured she was actually there. So much about Baird, Olive thought, was both theatrical *and* real. This was how Olive felt, too, as if she were both imagining and experiencing this, picking up a cue in a play and not performing, really living. She knew her part, she'd been preparing for it ever since she'd first heard Baird make a sound.

Now Olive sank to her knees on the floor before him. Abjectly, she kissed the small rock between his legs through the silk kimono, knowing exactly how though she'd never done it before. She began to part the paisley sides that concealed him and tug the soft belt he had tied with a bow.

But Baird stopped her and held her hand. He shook his head in a calm, mature, and disapproving way. He said, "Not now, not like this," like a small-town Midwestern father in a film finding and saving his daughter from sin. Tipping his head, he signaled her back to a standing position and then over to the chair from which she'd risen.

Then Baird spoke again.

"I've been cursed," he said.

"You have?"

"Yes."

"To do what?"

"To sing and be alone."

Baird said he had been a star many times, under different names, years and years before, over centuries, in other ages. Most recently, he had been Tony Cantare in the forties. He had never been able to cease, been sentenced to drift and never die. It hadn't been his idea, it had been imposed on him by the devil. The only thing that could stop him was the love of a loyal woman, and he'd always been betrayed. He was staring at Olive now, for she was the one for whom he'd been waiting.

And wait was what he wanted them both to do.

"To be sure," he said.

"Sure of what?" Olive was dizzy. This was a dream. Yet it was so real—and taking so long!

"Sure of you. Of us."

Seeing her off at the motel door, Baird kissed her hand, a suitably and frustratingly chivalrous gesture. Olive was dropped off at home by Baird's driver. This time, she had ridden in the back like an esteemed guest. Deadened as usual by work, Olive's parents had not waited up for her. That night, Olive frantically masturbated, her hands nearly causing a flame below and above her waist. The next day, she called in sick to school.

Olive waited to be contacted by Baird, which he said he'd do soon, after his next series of shows. In the meantime, her vow of fidelity—and, for now, celibacy—allowed her to refuse Dooley without explanation the next time he sought to sleep with her. She even kept her hand to herself.

"I don't get it," Dooley said.

"I don't need a reason," Olive said, moving farther away on the bed, feeling newly emboldened by her newly powerful position in Baird's life.

Dooley lay back, directly beneath the poster of the

Steely Dan album cover with the large female lips (all the kids knew their name meant dildo). At first, he sighed with what seemed suppressed rage. Then, surprising Olive, Dooley just shrugged. Smirking, he sat up, his open denim shirt revealing a beefy, only selectively haired chest.

"I bet this is about him," Dooley said.

"Who?"

"Baird Melody. That bourgeois, corporate…"

And he cursed what used to be called a blue streak. This was the harshest Dooley had ever been about Baird, yet his voice shook not only with anger. Olive realized Dooley was not just entitled and imperious but offended and injured. This made her like him less and—for the first time—fear him.

Dooley stood and tucked in and re-buttoned his shirt, tightening a belt he had not entirely undone. He seemed finished with Olive—for the day? Forever? It was hard to say.

"By the way," Dooley said, "I had a friend deliver a message to your idol. It said you were a slut. I admit, I was stoned when I wrote it, and my friend didn't know it was even in her envelope. But anyway."

Then Dooley strode from the room, leaving the door open, which said: *You can let yourself out.*

Olive assumed Dooley's friend was Miss Aker,

whom she knew had written Baird to thank him for spending time with the essay winners. When she made it to the mud room, she found her bike was gone. Outside, Olive saw it had been tossed past the lawn by Dooley, landing hard on the tiles near the swimming pool. One tire rim had been bent out of shape, and it rubbed against the wheel all the way home, one reason it took her longer than usual to get there. The other: Olive was crying too hard to see where she was headed.

Olive's attempts to reach Baird were for naught: she never got past the first level of his security. She even called the Jolly Roger motel, to learn the pseudonym under which he had registered. She was met with indifference and hostility, even when she began to hyperventilate.

At last, after class, Olive gathered her courage to confront the person who had inadvertently exposed Olive's lack of loyalty, the disclosure that had driven Baird from her life. Her beautiful blue eyes welling up under her Indian bandana, Miss Aker only stared blankly at her in the empty classroom, seeming to harbor a new grudge against Olive she would not explain.

"I have no idea what you're talking about," she said.

Weeks later, after school had let out for the summer, Olive learned that Miss Aker and Dooley had eloped, since he had just turned eighteen. Their destination was unknown; even his influential parents had no knowledge of where they had gone.

Later that season, hundreds of concertgoers were injured at Baird's concert in England after the stage collapsed. A fourteen-year-old girl was killed. At first, Baird's publicist claimed she had a heretofore unknown heart condition. Eventually, he admitted, once a coroner's report was leaked, that she had died of "traumatic asphyxia," or being crushed to death. Baird retreated to his mansion in Los Angeles, sending a cryptic message about having been "betrayed." Soon he was hospitalized for a drug overdose.

Olive expelled a breath, which seemed to contain the one white key of Baird's piano being struck over and over. Then the sounds of the seventies were submerged by the notes of Fyfe Moreso's new song, still coming from her device.

And there he was, Fyfe Moreso. His concert was over and he was looking through the screen at Olive. There was no one else around and nothing else between them. Fyfe began to speak.

"Save me."

He said he'd been cursed. He had been a star many times, under different names, years and years before, over centuries, in other ages. He said…

"Fyfe," Olive cut in.

…he had been Tony Cantare in the forties. Baird Melody in the seventies…

"Fyfe," she said. "Let me stop you there."

…and he had always been betrayed. Fyfe, who had been talking the whole time, suddenly became aware of what Olive had said.

"What?"

"I already know," she told him.

"You do? Oh."

Fyfe just sat there for a second, staring, at once relieved and disappointed that his big speech, over which he'd obviously slaved, had been unnecessary. Now it was Olive's turn to deliver a monologue. She told Fyfe what she had experienced when his song got inside her, the trip to their mutual past. When she paused to catch her breath, Fyfe tried to start up again, but she beat him to it.

"I'm good for it," Olive said. "I'll stick by you forever if you do the same for me. I'll never let you down."

There was a beat before Fyfe felt safe to respond, which he did in silence. He just wore a broader smile than Olive had ever seen on him. Suddenly, he looked like a normal person, even if his actual age was somewhere in three digits. Olive pressed a button and transferred his image from her device to the screen in her room. Then she stood.

Olive loved him then. They loved each other. She felt the cold glass of the screen against herself and pressed flatter on it to feel more. It was not the burning sensation she had imagined with his hologram, it was better, like ice on her bare skin, for she had removed everything above her waist. Then she undid and dropped what was below her belt and felt that go cold, as well, felt what was within her freeze on the screen, all over Fyfe's face, above and below what little beard he could grow. "I love you," she said, for the first time in her life to anyone.

Then there was a knock at the door.

Olive turned. Both she and Fyfe were panting, her torso stuck to the screen like something petrified on a windowsill by snow. Fyfe was half out of whatever he'd been wearing too.

Olive clutched her clothes. She didn't know whether to tell Fyfe to "hold on," which was ridiculous, or to answer whoever had come calling. Her father was still out of town, seeking talent—wasn't he? So, who could be outside, in the hall?

Olive pulled on her jeans and stuffed her panties in her pocket.

"Hold on!"

Olive had said this to the visitor, for Fyfe was now just in a tiny box on the bottom of the screen. He'd ducked out though not disappeared, the way freaked-out lovers once hid in closets or high-tailed it out windows onto ledges.

"Don't go anywhere," she said absurdly to the box. Then she opened the door. Starker Braun was there.

Olive stepped back. Stark wore the same stained and obscenely embossed T-shirt as he had in the church. He seemed like something that had crawled out of a grave after being buried. Yet it made sense: he was the reason Olive was not out of state, seeing and loving Fyfe in person. Stark had known she'd be home, since he had kept her there.

"Hi!" he said, as if his arrival was the most natural thing on Earth. "Can I *come in*?" he asked, as if having already been made to wait too long. "Thank you, I will." Then he crossed the threshold, snottily accepting the offer she hadn't made.

"What do you want?" Olive asked, her heart pounding from the excitement she'd felt with Fyfe. "And how did you get in?" Olive was afraid too.

Stark only shrugged, and she remembered how he'd broken into his father's house. Was there a little dirt and blood on his knuckles? Maybe.

As he limped closer, Olive glanced behind her, at the

screen. She knew that, even invisible, Fyfe could still see and hear Stark.

"Look," Stark said, "I think we should talk this out, because there's a lot for us to unpack."

To Olive's greater surprise, Stark doubled down on the heartfelt desire he had shown her at the church, before he cursed and threatened her, of course. He spoke as if they'd had a spat and things had been left unsaid, and he wished to rectify that. Olive realized that, like many isolated people, Stark had been going over and over this situation without input from others, so his fantasies had become facts, because they had never been contradicted, for no one with any sense wanted anything to do with him, which only made Stark *more* isolated and *more* engaged with his obsessions, which pushed even *more* people away, and so on and so on, until he had come to the carefully considered conclusion that he had to be in Olive's room, right now.

"I mean," he said, "we've meant so much to each other."

Stark was sincere, and this made him extra scary for he was standing next to Olive, probably capable of violence, and he could convince Fyfe, who was still remotely present, that what he was saying was true.

"What do you think," Stark asked, "about all this?"

The question had been uttered because Olive had

said nothing, hadn't even made eye contact with him, and even someone as dissociative as Stark could take the hint. As Stark had before—and would, she knew, continue to do until he lashed out—he grew emotional.

"I love you," he said. "And I know you feel something for me. Don't deny it!"

In the space of three sentences, Stark had gone from open and affectionate to defensive and demanding, and Olive could predict where he was headed next. Yet she couldn't focus on Stark. She was only concerned that Fyfe would think she'd been—in the old-fashioned parlance of the story to which he and she had been sentenced—untrue.

"It's untrue!" she said, turning to the TV.

But the bottom of the screen was blank, and Fyfe was gone. All that was left was an old still of the star, a remnant of the way Olive used to love him, before she knew how much they meant to each other, when she'd been young.

In the other iterations of their story, Olive's sort-of boyfriends had been openly antagonistic toward the singer. Stark, however, was a man of his time and cared only about his own anguish, his own anger, and couldn't be bothered to bully Fyfe. Stark looked over Olive's shoulder at the screen.

"Hey," he said, with curiosity, "it's that singer."

Stark glanced at the publicity photo of Fyfe, in which he grinned, semi-nude and disturbingly thin. Then he shifted to Olive, whose eyes were obscured by tears filling, flooding, and overflowing them, falling between her lips and drowning her in her desire for Fyfe. Stark's own eyes grew wide. You mean, he was being rejected *again* and for *Fyfe Moreso*? That was ridiculous!

"*What*?" was all he succeeded in saying.

Then Stark's limited view of the world expanded. His world was invaded, to be exact, as if by killer birds in an old movie he'd seen once on the watch of someone beside him on a train. Olive dived at him, flapping, slapping, scratching, and even—he couldn't be sure but it hurt like hell—biting, sending Stark back on his heels. She was a great, angry gull, screaming, crying, cawing and hooting, pushing him past the threshold of the open door into the hall. There she sent him still farther until he reached the first step of the staircase on which he slipped and—seeing Olive stay on and recede from the top—sailed down like the guy in that psycho movie by the same director. This was the last image Stark saw before he hit the runner on the first floor and the impact emptied his head of everything.

Zombie-like, Olive retreated into her room. There she tried to contact Fyfe, though no method she knew reaped any results. She was left just with the same frozen images and facsimiles as before. At last, she looked for a way to join him wherever he'd gone.

From a drawer, she retrieved a commemorative CD she'd been sent by a Fyfe website for reaching a milestone of fandom, a million views of a video. Olive had never opened the case, for she had no way to play it, no one did; it was as archaic to her as the radio and broadcast TV beloved by her earlier incarnations. It had been simply decorative. Now it had a purpose.

Olive opened it, smashing against her desk the cheap glass case that covered Fyfe's soulful face on the booklet liner notes. The pieces were small yet sharp enough to cut the skin below her palm which lay like a film of dew over the snaking river of her pulse. If nothing else, Olive thought, this would lift the curse, and free the two of them, in an after-life.

Then came a new knock on the door.

"Olive!"

Lorne had arrived home early. He hadn't seen Starker emerge a minute earlier from the house, bleeding, barely conscious, speaking unintelligibly, walking the wrong way toward his church basement. He'd find the broken window later.

Neither Lorne nor Olive knew that Fyfe Moreso

was committing suicide at the same time, leaving the word *betrayal* on a tablet.

Regaining consciousness in the hospital, Olive knew that she had a father somewhere, but that was all she remembered. It took her a minute to fight through drugs and realize Lorne was standing by her bed.

"It wasn't the tabling of my good news, my *great* news," he was saying. "That wasn't the worst part. It was your suicide attempt. I mean, my finding you just in time." Lorne was pacing, rattled by events, talking to himself as much as her. "Who knew you were so obsessed with that stupid singer? Well, anyway, Fyfe is over, finished. I got a much better person for the party." He mentioned someone whose name Olive didn't catch. "That was my good news, my great news, ruined by Fyfe and your Romeo and Juliet routine. I mean, I never saw the original but I saw the musical comedy cartoon with the cat and dog, with the new, better, happier ending. It's like the happy ending I created by saving your life! I saved the day but secretly, not crowing about it. So, I have to be satisfied with being a good Samaritan—a great!"

Olive began to pass out again. As she did, she looked up at headlines rushing like racecars across an elevated video screen she could not turn off. Among the streaming sentences, one stood out like a fancy private sedan among drab, self-driving vehicles.

"Singing star Fyfe Moreso rumored to survive health scare."

When Olive woke up alone, she thought she might have imagined it. Weakly, she went on her own device and learned the story had been unsourced gossip about Fyfe, an irresponsible insinuation like so much so-called news now. Then a private message suggested otherwise.

It wasn't a message in so many words or any words at all. It was a texted image of Baird Melody singing at the Coliseum, the outdoor Long Island arena in the seventies. Olive learned that the venue had long since been replaced by a giant condominium that stood in the field it had obliterated. (It had been many things over the decades since the seventies, including a ranch for lab-grown cows, pigs, and other once-real, now artificial yet still edible animals.) Scribbled beside the picture were the number and letter "67A" after a pound sign. Was it an apartment number? That's what it seemed like.

By the end of the week, prescribed sedatives, Olive was discharged from care. Outside the hospital, a self-driving car had been sent to take her home. Olive overrode the computer's instructions and gave it a new address, far from her father's house.

As happened so often now, seasons seemed to shift by the second on the drive. It occurred in heat and cold, bright sun and storm-wracked clouds, with umbrellas up and down, scarves on and off, sweat drenching and dried. By the time she arrived, Olive felt years older but filled with a new and child-like hope.

The car let her out at the seventy-story condo that had replaced the Coliseum. Olive rode the endless elevator up. On the apartment door—67A—she believed was Fyfe's, a flier had been pasted sloppily and askew with some unidentified sticky substance. It featured a crude color stock photo of fingers on piano keys. *Come hear Effe Smeoro!* it screamed, a horrible or maybe just hasty anagram of the superstar's names. *One night only!* The address was a nightclub in the Farmer's Loop Mall, one of few spaces still occupied in the nearby, nearly deserted structure.

The club was part of a chain, a free-state-only group of low-rent performing spaces designed to showcase up-and-coming or down-and-out artists. "Talent" would pay for the privilege and split the nonexistent profits with management, a company called Your Last Act, meant to acknowledge the culmination of these artists' years-long efforts to be seen and celebrated.

This was where Olive thought she might find Fyfe.

"One, please," Olive said into the mic at the stylized circular imitation ticket booth outside, manned by a bow-tied animatronic clerk, which scanned her irises and took her temperature before dispensing an old-school "ducat," as the hypoallergenic skin-thin piece of paper was called.

Inside was a narrow, dark, and unpleasantly aromatic cabaret. Replacing a conventional audience was a small collection of computers from which virtual customers watched. The Illness Index today was Perfectly Decent (PD): any threat came from the place's rampant uncleanliness, not rampaging disease. Olive was the only human there, sitting on a splintered stool in utter darkness before a trap door-sized stage lit by a single bulb. She'd heard there was an unwritten law in theater: if there were more people onstage than in the house, actors didn't have to go on. Seeing just dark screens around her, Olive assumed today the numbers would be tied at one.

Head-bendingly loud rock music blurted from a lone speaker, and the bulb cast a skinny spotlight on the center of the stage. A figure entered, raising a hand to block his eyes from the light obscuring his face. Sitting on a stool before a piano, the only instrument, he shifted sideways, as if to collect himself, and remained anonymous. When he abruptly began to play, he dipped his face so close to the keys it was as if he were kissing or even consuming them. His fingers slid this way and that, creating something as near to music as a mere rattling of black and white wood. Then he bent back so far, he was perpendicular to the piano, another way to stay unseen, stared straight up and screamed as much as sang to the ceiling. He bowed his head and spun completely around on the stool, blurring his features as he revolved.

Then he stopped, face front. He began to burp out his first—and Olive, hoped, only—song. He didn't look at her, didn't see an audience at all, stared above and beyond her eyeline. If she'd hoped he'd be identifiable now that his features weren't obscured, she was wrong. Yet the way he was *still* unrecognizable made Olive know it was Fyfe.

There was a shifting, static-y field where his face should have been, the old fuzzy snow of poor reception, even the occasional flash of a test pattern, as if his station had gone off the air, seen and unseen by Olive, subliminal, as in old ads. All along, Fyfe's sounds—the song he was supposed to be "selling"—fluctuated frustratingly from the forties of Tony to the seventies of Baird right up to Fyfe's own oeuvre. But if *that* catalogue had been intentional and artistic, a kind of collage, this was merely a mistake, a malfunction, nothing but noise.

Fyfe's eyes drifted from neutral nether-parts in the air to Olive and caught her stare, locked in on her like a pilot landing, not going anywhere else. She took the opportunity.

"Fyfe!" she cried at full volume, for no one else was there.

Fyfe blinked and gurgled once while gushing out his greatest hits. Then he kept going. Olive could see in the opacity of his eyes that he was, for all intents and purposes, asleep.

He finally finished, which meant he closed his mouth mid-flat-and-sharp note. He didn't wait for a reaction: Fyfe turned and stomped offstage, raising and dropping his feet dramatically, like a soldier drilled for decades to do so. Olive attempted to appreciate him, cheering and applauding, calling his name and bellowing "bravo!" or as close to a bellow as her body could expel. After an uncertain second, the lights went off, first slowly and then all at once, the way they say societies cease to exist.

Olive stumped into the unilluminated aisle, colliding with chairs and dashing at least one device to the floor before she made her way out. In the little lobby, she found Fyfe, who was now barely anyone for more than a minute at a time. He stood, waiting for someone, he wasn't sure who. Seeing her, he knew it was Olive.

Fyfe shivered, as if casting off a cowl that covered him completely. Then he seemed to step out of something. He lifted one foot after the other and let them fall to the floor, his mess of identities an unsightly slip he peeled off and kicked away. He no longer looked clad in a stupid amount of iconic costumes—punk, cowboy, or whatever—draped over him by a diabolical dresser. The static that was fuzzing his features disappeared. Fyfe was in focus and awake.

"You," he said.

"Yes. Me."

"Olive."

He knew her name, maybe had been reminded of it by Tony or Baird or how many other enslaved singers were inside him. She didn't ask where he'd been or how he'd survived. She only intended, as the old expression went, to nip this in the bud.

Olive came close. She turned up her palms, exposing the scars from the shattered CD cover. It was amazing the damage it had done, given it was made of cheap glass. It was like the impact of his sentimental songs over centuries, she thought. You couldn't believe how much they'd meant to people.

"Wow," he said. "Are you all right?"

"Now I am."

Nearly nose to nose, Olive looked for scars on him, too, but saw none: his skin was as pale and porcelain as before. Had Fyfe's rumored "attempt" not been for real? Then Olive realized the faint ring around his neck was no choker or tattoo but the evidence of a blade that had gone in a complete circle, like an old-fashioned can opener turned to the end of a tin. Olive raised her volume so there'd be no mistake.

"I've never," she said, "been unfaithful."

The information roused him, like a slap or cold water or whatever was thrown at a face in old movies. Fyfe reached out and took her hand. Olive felt they didn't stop running until they reached his house and apartment 67A. There Fyfe yanked the flier from his door as they went in.

High above everything, the two-room apartment was barely furnished: boxes of memorabilia were overflowing or unopened in corners; clothes still on hangars were piled up on the floor. It looked less like a place a superstar would stay than a perpetual traveler's pitstop or a terrorist's safe house, somewhere to stash stuff or stay hidden.

They didn't, couldn't wait. Within an instant, Olive and Fyfe were on that floor, his pants, her skirt, both sets of their drawers dropped and chucked aside. Olive had never actually made love with a real person, just with pictures and approximations. Now it felt like three men were naked with her, Tony, Baird, and Fyfe, and he was hard enough for all of them. She held them as they pushed, pulled back, and pumped, in an orgy inside her. Their chorus said they loved her and she came one, two, three times. As they finished, they cried out in every voice they had. Then Olive was alone with Fyfe, who had faded to be only himself for the first time.

Now that the curse had been lifted, they put his stuff away. Fyfe marveled at Olive's method of cleaning up, which was normal if maybe a bit more precise than other people's. She realized: both as a celebrity and someone cursed to be re-born through time, Fyfe had never done much housework.

"Keep?" he asked, holding up a hideous half-knight-in-armor, half nun's wimple pullover. "Or throw away?"

"Throw away," she said, and he did as he was told.

Olive never asked why he'd come to this place. Fyfe had probably just drifted there chasing a suppressed memory, in the same somnambulance she'd helped him to end. There was still no furniture other than an old ottoman left by the last tenant, which looked like a severed foot in a black leather boot, Olive thought. So, they ate take-out on the floor and made love there before and after meals. Fyfe was starting to find himself as one lover and not an assortment and Olive was getting used to hugging, kissing, sucking, and licking someone's actual flesh, as opposed to that on screens or in dreams. Fyfe was still so slight, lean, and hairless he made Olive feel porcine and hirsute by comparison. Yet…

"I love all of this," Fyfe whispered, surprising himself by begging her to nearly suffocate himself with her breasts. "The so much," he said, barely articulate. "That's what I want."

"Good," she said. "Because that's what I've got."

"Come close to killing me with you," he said, and she did, his nails digging into her, becoming their code for letting him loose and making sure he survived.

"I love that," he said, panting, his face red.

"Me too."

Still, Olive noticed there was a kind of neutrality to this inaugural Fyfe. She often had to initiate things, for he was noncommittal. Was he simply learning to live or did he lack the imagination to offer any opinions? Olive didn't want to judge him; she just longed to love him.

"I'll tell you what I want," he said, as if addressing this, though she hadn't asked him, late one night, while he lay nearly asleep beside her.

"What's that?" she said.

"To marry you."

Olive didn't reply before he passed out. She waited for him to repeat himself the next day, in case it had just been a sleepy reverie he wouldn't remember. Yet almost immediately in the morning, he asked…

"So, what do you think?"

"About what?"

"Marriage."

"Oh."

The admittedly endearing idea was also banal. While sweet and sincere, Olive thought, it was often the go-to for an uninspired man early in an affair.

"Maybe wait?" she said. "I mean, we just got here." And she meant it both literally and figuratively.

"Even…if we love each other?"

Again, Olive paused. She didn't want to offend him. Yet she wondered: as a new immigrant to the land of normal existence, was Fyfe trying to figure everything out and fit in, as if misspeaking slang the second he was sworn in as a citizen? Or was this who he actually was? In other words, did he know better? Or not? It made Olive like him a little more but want him a little less. Yet how could she hurt him by saying no? Wouldn't that get everything off on the wrong foot? It was a problem.

"Well…" she said, feeling cowardly but again unclear what else to do, "we could try?"

Of course, there was no trying, they had to do. Olive hoped to stall by asking to arrange something she didn't want to have happen.

"Who should we invite?" she asked.

"What do you mean?"

"To the circus. I mean, cervix. I mean, service." She was anxious.

"Like...relatives?"

"Yes."

Olive felt funny about contacting her own family. She had only let Lorne know she was alive in a quick text the night after arriving. ("Everything's fine," it had said, and been an after-thought.) The idea of telling anyone about her marrying Fyfe was unappealing. Keeping the relationship a secret was exciting, something that was hers alone. Or did she want to wait for another reason she couldn't say, even to herself?

Luckily, Fyfe's face went pale at the prospect of inviting people related to him. Who were they? Were there any?

"Um," he said, "let's not."

"Okay!" she said, perhaps too quickly.

"We'll just..." He turned on his device and conjured up a virtual wedding ceremony with an A.I. witness, their own avatars, artificial signatures, and images of rings, gowns, tuxes, and rice. Vows had already been written, and they tweaked them just a little, for every alteration cost. Fyfe disinfected the screen before they kissed the lips of their computer-generated selves.

They intended to "honeymoon" in the neighborhood but quickly learned there was almost nothing outside the massive complex in which they lived. Inside, however, on the lobby floor, were restaurants of all cuisines, shops of every sort, live entertainment venues, and sports arenas. It was "Weather-Secured and Germ-Disinfected TM, for comfort during any climate or disease possibility."

Soon Olive grew tired of these unending opportunities to eat, watch, and play. She felt as seasick as a passenger on a cruise ship, a vehicle she had always refused to board when Lorne booked them tickets. Fyfe, on the other hand, could not get enough of the—Olive thought—generic and bland food and fun vetted by corporations and moguls.

"It's all so great," he said, as starry-eyed as a small child, "isn't it?"

At night, when they returned from these—Olive thought—billionaire-approved and celebrity-stamped revels, Fyfe was too fatigued to do much else. Olive had hoped their "honeymoon" would be one in more than name only, the occasion for nightly if not all-daily explorations of their physical and animal selves. Yet when she convinced Fyfe to come to bed, still on the floor—and she had to, it was always up to her—Fyfe seemed to consider it an obligation if not a courtesy, and for him, not them both. Now, the bury-me-in-your-breasts act was not a helplessly and breathlessly begged-for event, almost unbearably erotic and endlessly changed, refined, and improved, but a ritualized routine done the same way every time and the only way they each ever touched the other, as if no other ways existed. Olive was too shy and frankly inexperienced to suggest something different; it was all up to Fyfe, and he wouldn't do it.

At last, the honeymoon ended, even though they still lived in the same place and could have continued it forever. It was Fyfe's decision. Her new husband believed there was a time and place for everything, and now was the time for something besides fun.

"I better get a job," he said.

"What?"

"A guy's got to work."

Once more, Olive held her tongue. She had assumed as a music superstar, Fyfe had made inexhaustible amounts of money, the apartment itself, which he had mentioned buying in cash, eliminating the need for a mortgage, was evidence. Yet Olive learned how he judged the very idea of jobbing.

"It's the right thing to do," he said.

"It is?"

"Yes. A man can't just sit and do nothing."

Olive was about to suggest that Fyfe had a natural gift with which he'd always be able to make a living. Yet, knowing where she was "going with this," he shot her the time-honored look that signaled, *Don't start.*

"But…"

He gave her the look again.

Olive hadn't known that lifting the curse by being loyal to Fyfe would mean he might abandon music altogether. He had, in fact, been humming around their home so off-key she wondered if he'd always been helped by auto-tune. His image would occasionally appear online with a caption like *Where flew the songbird?* Had he become so different he was no longer known by anyone, even himself? Maybe, Olive thought.

Fyfe began to follow leads for a new occupation, going on employment sites, filling out applications, and making follow-up calls. Within a week, undeniably excited, he told her…

"I got it."

"Got what?"

"The job I told you about."

"Oh!"

Maybe Olive had just not wanted to hear, but she

had completely forgotten. Fyfe turned his device toward her, as if unwrapping a gift.

"You're talking to the new…" he began, and Olive read the rest.

"Altered Images and Augmented Sounds Coordinator, Music Event Division, Diversified Enterprises."

"DE" had been the logo on most of the lobby diversions, Olive remembered. She could manage a—maybe excessively broad, even maniacal-looking—smile but no words. Then…

"Congrats," she released, like a final breath.

"Thanks! It's a great opportunity. Sky's the limit."

"But…didn't they recognize your name, Fyfe Moreso?"

"Well…" Fyfe looked offended that she was in the dark. "I gave my real name, not my stage one."

When she didn't nod or offer it up, for she'd never known it, Fyfe "reminded" her in an affectionate yet condescending way. The name was so normal, so typical, so generic it immediately left her mind, and she didn't know it again. Brown? Jones? Miller? Something.

"There's a celebration downstairs tonight," he said, thrilled, "at the Brew-Ha-Ha. For all the new hires. Except for drinks and dessert, it's on DE!"

Olive considered "having a headache" but Fyfe swiftly began offering advice on what she should wear, even combing through her closet and laying out an ensemble on the new bed he'd recently bought, after complaining of back pains from the floor, their love-making there unmentioned. He tugged insinuatingly at the back of Olive's hair, implying it was time for a trim.

"'Hairy's is open until seven downstairs," Fyfe said, referencing the salon next to the ten-minute movie theater.

Olive didn't go for a haircut, but she was made so self-conscious about her appearance that she ran late for the event, coaxed impatiently by Fyfe to hurry, after she'd changed outfits and hair partings too many times.

"Let's go, let's go," he said, patting her behind to get her out the door. "The race is to the swift."

Downstairs, Olive met the Bollocks, Mac and Ginger, and the Cobblers, Trina and Tick. The six of them were bound to reconnoiter often in each other's homes, since all except Olive worked for DE. This first night, Olive was told what position each held but—like Fyfe's name—she forgot right away. Yet Fyfe was in his element, kibitzing with the couples, names, places, and events from their workplace, flying at full speed without explanations for Olive who, to be fair, never asked for any. Only of interest to Olive: no one seemed to know Fyfe was anything but a new employee. His fame had evaporated along with, it seemed, his talent for and interest in music.

Fyfe poured himself into his new job, which was to digitally alter the words and music of playlists piped into DE's countless locations in order to avoid paying royalties. (Olive thought this was his job, she wasn't sure.) It was a practice she believed Fyfe, Tony, and Baird would have decried in their old lives. She offered no opinion, so Fyfe blithely assumed her support.

Yet Olive's disquiet didn't go entirely unnoticed. Mac Bollocks, one of the couples' gang with whom they socialized, approached her during a cookout in the Cobblers' backyard (Trina and Tick had bought a home in a suburb DE had recently refurbished, and it was their turn to host). A drink in hand, Mac, like Olive, hovered near an electric grill on which hot dogs made from the ear cells of living pigs were roasting.

"Quit judging," he said, not completely serious.

"I'm not." Olive was taken aback and pointed to the smoking kind-of-meat. "It looks delicious." She was also not too serious.

"That's not what I meant."

"No? What am I judging?"

"Everything."

Mac swallowed the liquid left in his glass, then sucked, tongued, and juggled two pieces of ice. Raising and lowering his eyebrows, he walked away.

Olive remembered: Mac was the sort-of-acerbic one, a quality which had made him sort-of stand out from the other employee pals. To her surprise, Olive realized Mac had been right about her, and her face went hot red, and not just from the pigs' ear smoke.

Maybe, Olive thought, Fyfe was too busy with his own unhappiness to worry about hers. She began to notice a certain slackening of his resolve about work and a lassitude in his behavior in general. The amounts of beers and other kinds of booze he drank at cook-outs and cocktail parties with the DE crowd began to increase. Fyfe seemed to chug-a-lug in a manic not a merry manner, not to blow off steam but to bury mis-givings.

"Are you all right?" Olive would ask when he'd stumble getting out of the elevator or trip on easily avoided objects on their floor.

"I'm fine!" he'd yell back, as if aware of and guilty about how off-kilter he was.

"I'm just trying to help," she'd say, knowing she should just shut up.

"Well, stop helping!" he'd holler.

"Okay, okay," she'd reply, for the violence in his voice upset her.

Now, in the rare times he came close to her in bed or let her at least try to caress him, Fyfe was incapable of performing, which only increased his anger, and he would curl up, inconsolable, at a distance from her on the mattress (an even bigger one he'd recently ordered without consulting her). One day, while making up the bed with old sheets she found weren't large enough to cover its great expanse, which guaranteed, of course, greater distance between them, Olive found empty pill bottles stashed with prescriptions written in a foreign language, possibly Russian. Next to them was a printed-out news item about a supposed sighting of Fyfe Moreso—"Is this the warbler's ghost?"—with a furtive photo of a scrawny, bearded, homeless man who bore a passing resemblance to Fyfe. Her husband seemed to have saved it the way one would a story about a secret celebrity crush.

All of this told Olive that Fyfe agreed with her unspoken assessment that this new life was limited, dull, and frustrating. His reactions had been no worse than that of many men—sodden, angry, and inexpressive. If he didn't beat Olive, he had come close once when he stumbled drunkenly into her, knocking her into a wall with a muttered and unmeant apology. His silences and lack of openness informed Olive, too, that if he didn't actively blame her, he felt he couldn't speak to her, that she'd never understand.

Olive did blame herself. She believed she'd put

a new curse on Fyfe, doomed him to normalcy, to a good paying job, a young, loving wife, and mortality, which, he was proving, was worse for him than singing through centuries, unloved and alone. It was a personal thing; it wouldn't have been the same for everybody.

"I'm sorry," she whispered to Fyfe one night in bed, convinced he was unconscious, for he'd been so smashed at the Bollocks' boat bash he'd fallen overboard.

"For what?" he whispered, suddenly, and Olive was too startled to say. Then she blurted out…

"For everything," which was what Mac had answered when asked what Olive had been judging. Fyfe grunted and shrugged, as if agreeing she was at fault and it was too late, but he forgave her, anyway, though he was probably just swallowing phlegm before passing out again.

Yet what could she do? To betray Fyfe, she couldn't go back to Stark, for that would be a worse punishment of her than it would ever be of him. She was frozen in mid-air in their home, like an icicle at the top of a tree, loving and still loyal to a figment of Fyfe from which both needed to be freed. She couldn't reach out to Lorne: she was too embarrassed; she had never told him anything. Olive knew only the people with whom Fyfe worked, who weren't even her own friends. What did any of them even know about her?

"Everything," she heard Mac say again, and even if it wasn't true, even if he knew next to nothing about her, it was not nothing, and so it was enough.

For their next group outing, they had arranged to meet for a game of Fatch at a stadium in the lobby. Fyfe watched from the stands, plastic beer cup grasped with both hands. The new sport combined Fetch and Catch, with one contestant playing human, the other dog. Olive found the competition odd and only took on the canine role after losing a virtual coin toss. Yet sprinting on all fours across artificial turf, she found freedom in the purely physical experience, imagined she was emptying her anxiety in the waterfall of sweat flowing off her. She even shut her eyes, galloping forward, pretending the perspiration was sponging away what saddened and scared her, a rain or a river washing it into tributaries or gutters or wherever cleansing water went, she didn't know.

Then Olive smashed into stone.

She went rolling over and over with another player, whose muscled frame had been the block into which she had slammed. When she opened her eyes, she was in her own bed, the other person staring down at her, concerned.

"At last," Mac Bollocks said. "There she is."

For the first time, compassion mixed with his usual good-natured nastiness. Had she done it all on purpose? Hadn't there been a better or just less bruising way to see him? Or had self-punishment been the point?

"The doctor said to call him if you woke up," he said.

Mac's hair was still moist and flattened on his brow, and his shorts and T-shirt stuck to his torso, so she hadn't been unconscious for that long.

"Don't bother about the doctor," she said. "I'm fine."

"You sure?"

"Yes."

"Okay. If you say so."

"I do."

Olive squirmed on the oversized mattress, which felt as big as the field on which she'd crashed and been concussed. Her own shirt and shorts were clammy. The space between her eyes throbbed.

"Where's Fyfe?" She realized from Mac's dumb expression he had always addressed her husband by his real name. Mac must have assumed hers was some marital love name, because he shrugged and said…

"In the other room. Dead to the world." He made a drinking gesture and then simulated sleep.

Olive nodded. Then she peeled down her shorts and

her underwear went, too, stuck to them by sweat. The cool air felt exciting on her bare skin, and she spread her legs to get the full effect. All the while, she smiled at Mac. Her smell was so strong, Olive was sure he perceived it, and it was one more thing that further opened his eyes.

Mac's cynicism and ever-present smirk were now replaced by surprise and innocence. He was about to ask whether Olive was sure about doing this, Fyfe being in the next room—Olive assumed he was about to, anyway—but she stopped him by reaching for his hand. She made him put as many fingers as he could inside her, which turned out to be two. This made him whisper...

"It's going to be good between us."

Soon his own shorts were at his thighs, and she had him take them off, so there'd be no turning back.

"Don't whisper," she said, at full voice. "Let's be as loud as we can."

Olive was surprised how much she wanted him—how lonely she was, how miserable her marriage—this was no mere means to an end. She liked Mac, as much as she knew of him, sensed his snideness was a shield. There was more to know of him, at least, which you couldn't say about everyone. In bed, he wasn't only eager, he was almost entranced. Mac waited for her to finish, then came, too, obeying her orders to be as loud as he liked. Then…

"Everything about you is interesting," he said.

Olive looked over his slowly lowering shoulders and saw Fyfe in the doorway.

Though he looked momentarily menacing, Fyfe soon crumbled like the mean old witch who got the water thrown on her or whatever it was in the old movie. He seeped onto the floor, slowly, in sections, until he was as flimsy as a pile of clothes no one cared about enough to wash or throw away. When he was lifted by Mac, who had scrambled on his shorts, Fyfe clutched him to stay stable, then hugged him hard with both hands, grateful and not angry at all.

Fyfe never mentioned the incident. Yet it was clear to them both that the curse had been reimposed and their marriage was over. For a few days, Olive stayed nearly still in the apartment, wondering what to do, where, how and when to go. She was secretly waiting for Mac to call, for that would at least provide her an answer and option. When he didn't, Olive gave him the benefit of the doubt: he was guilty about or even traumatized by what had occurred. After all, she had seduced him for her own purposes and received a surprising amount of pleasure from it. So why would she be the one who felt hurt? Still, she was new at this—affairs, sex, love, at adulthood—and didn't want to judge herself or anyone else too harshly.

Olive noticed that Fyfe was calling in sick to DE more often, staying sober and singing on-key, proving he had always been talented and his talent had been hurt by the curse lifting, the curse had been crucial to his career and life. Some kinds of suffering were worse than others. Live and learn, Olive thought, understanding this expression for the first time.

When she finally packed up, left, and waited outside for the car she had called, Olive swore she could hear Fyfe singing boisterously from the sixty-seventh floor, like opera singers on balconies in other centuries or Broadway stars before open windows during pandemic lockdowns. But that was impossible—wasn't it?

Later that night, as the car approached her father's street, Olive saw vehicles parked outside for blocks and valets scrambling to move them back, forth, and sideways. The place was lit up as if by bombs exploding, and she could hear someone singing in screams through a loudspeaker. Olive was far enough away to wonder: Was Lorne's party in the past? Or in the future?

"It's okay," she programmed the driver. "I can walk from here."

Weeks later, Olive learned she was pregnant, not

knowing at first who the father was, Fyfe or Mac. She didn't like making an analogy between the different lives in Fyfe and the one now in her, for she felt it was cloying. Eventually, she accepted it as inevitable. At least it would be her own blessing, her own curse.

Book Club Discussion Questions

1) How does this new "Flying Dutchman" compare to the original legend?

2) How would you describe Olive (i.e. appealingly youthful, needs to grow up, etc.)?

3) What do you make of all the incarnations of Fyfe Moreso (Tony Cantare in the forties, Baird Melody in the seventies)?

4) Is the "lifting" of the curse a good thing for Fyfe? Bad? Something else?

5) In the end, what has Olive learned about love?